Stacey,

xoxo

- L.A.

NEW YORK TIMES & USA TODAY BESTSELLING AUTHOR
L. A. CASEY

Aideen
a slater brothers novella
Copyright © 2015 by L.A. Casey
Published by L.A. Casey
www.lacaseyauthor.com

Cover Design by Mayhem Cover Creations | Editing by JaVa Editing
Formatting by JT Formatting

This book is licensed for your personal enjoyment only. This book may not be re-sold or given away to other people. If you would like to share this book with another person, please purchase an additional copy for each recipient. If you're reading this book and did not purchase it, or it wasn't purchased for your use only, then please return to your favorite book retailer and purchase your own copy. Thank you for respecting the hard work of this author.
All rights reserved.
Except as permitted under S.I. No. 337/2011 – European Communities (Electronic Communications Networks and Services) (Universal Service and Users' Rights) Regulations 2011, no part of this publication may be reproduced, distributed, or transmitted in any form or by any means, or stored in a database or retrieval system, without prior written permission of the author. The scanning, uploading, and distribution of this book via the Internet or via other means without the permission of the publisher is illegal and punishable by law. Please purchase only authorized electronic editions and do not participate in or encourage electronic piracy of copyrighted materials. This is a work of fiction. Names, characters, places, brands, media, and incidents are either the product of the author's imagination or are used fictitiously. The author acknowledges the trademarked status and trademark owners of various products referenced in this work of fiction, which have been used without permission. The publication/use of these trademarks is not authorized, associated with, or sponsored by the trademark owners.

Aideen / L.A. Casey – 1st ed.
ISBN-13: 978-1518695094 | ISBN-10: 1518695094

Mary and Yessi,

You're both the craziest best friends a girl could ever have, but I wouldn't change either of you for the world. Thank you for the daily conversations that make me laugh, and for the funny shit you both have said when you try to be serious. I'll take some of those weird conversations to my grave.

I promise ;)

I love you both dearly,
Lee <3

Chapter One	1
Chapter Two	17
Chapter Three	33
Chapter Four	44
Chapter Five	55
Chapter Six	73
Chapter Seven	85
Chapter Eight	112
Preview of *Ryder*	129
Other Titles	140
Acknowledgments	141
About the Author	143

CHAPTER ONE

P ain.

Stomach pain.

Severe stomach pain.

That was what I was currently experiencing... and it was all because of a damn biscuit. If I didn't get the sugary, crunchy goodness into my rumbling belly soon I would go on a rampage that would put Nico Slater to shame.

"Keela, *please*," I whimpered, feeling close to tears. "Just give me a little bit of that biscuit, I won't tell—"

"Aideen!"

I winced when his voice filled the sitting room.

"Ah, bollocks," I muttered under my breath and avoided looking over to the doorway where I knew he stood.

Instead, I focused on the beautifully decorated Christmas tree that stood behind Keela.

Keela Daley—who was still my best friend for some strange reason—was sitting on my sofa and acting as a leg rest for my swollen limbs. Two days prior, the cast I wore on my broken leg for the past eight weeks was removed. My knee and shin were nicely healed, but they were still prone to damage so I had to take things easy, which meant I had to sit down a lot.

I wasn't exactly happy about the prospect of sitting on my arse twenty-four-seven, but if it helped my leg get stronger then it was something I would just have to do.

I glanced down to my forearm then, sighing at the newly formed scar. It healed a few weeks ago, and Kane assured me it was an angry reddish colour because it was brand new. Over time, it would fade to a lighter colour.

I hoped so, because I could see myself wearing a lot of long-sleeved tops in the future otherwise.

Keela regained my attention when she devilishly grinned at me as she popped the remainder of her chocolate digestive biscuit into her mouth—cunt move—then looked to the left and held up her hands. "I wasn't goin' to give her it, Kane. I swear."

I ignored my boyfriend's presence and focused on the bitch in front of me.

"You're a shitty friend."

She looked back to me and unapologetically shrugged her shoulders. "I'd rather be a shitty friend than a dead one."

I scoffed. "He wouldn't kill you for givin' me a bit of a biscuit—"

"He *would* kill her for giving you a biscuit." A husky voice cut me off.

I huffed in frustration and looked at the love of my life who was hell-bent on making me suffer. I locked my eyes on his and silently pleaded with him.

"It's been eight weeks since I left the hospital, Kane. *Eight weeks*. Me leg and arm have healed perfectly and me throat doesn't even hurt anymore. I'm sick to death of soup and soft foods. I'm pregnant which means I'm *always* hungry, and that shitty food isn't cuttin' it anymore. Please, just let me eat a packet of biscuits."

"A *whole* packet?" Keela merrily laughed. "You fat fuck. How did eatin' a single biscuit jump to eatin' a whole bloody packet?"

I dug the heel of my foot into her thigh. "Shut the hell up you traitorous cow!"

She hissed and adjusted my foot, but did as asked and closed her mouth.

"Aideen," Kane sighed and rubbed his temples.

He has done that action a lot over the past few weeks.

"I'm not being strict to upset you, babydoll, but you heard the doctor. No solid food until *after* your throat fully heals. You have just a few more days and then you're good. Why risk it? The first time you ate solid food after the fire you made a gash in your throat and it required stitches. Do you really want to go down that road again?"

Kane was firm when he spoke, but I saw the emotion in his eyes.

"Do you *want* to undergo more surgery, not being able to talk and having to eat through a tube? Personally, I can't see you in that state. It almost killed me the first time around."

I thought of the gut-wrenching moment seven weeks ago when I swallowed a bit of a ham sandwich and my throat erupted with pain. A single slice of hard-crusted bread caused my already sensitive inner throat to tear open. It resulted in a painful gash that led to me spitting up a horrifying amount of blood that frightened the life out of those who loved me. I made Gavin and the girls cry, and I almost gave Kane and my father a heart attack.

To be honest, I scared myself half to death, too.

The pain after the surgery to stitch the wound shut, and having to be fed through a tube, sucked. I was a mess for weeks. It was definitely something I never wanted to experience again.

Ever.

I looked to Kane, then to Keela, then down to my fingers that were playing with the fluffy blanket that covered both Keela and myself.

"No, I don't," I replied to Kane, but made sure to keep my head and gaze downcast so he couldn't see that my eyes had welled up.

I hated how easily I cried at things.

Pregnancy turned me into such a pussy.

"Baby?" Kane prompted.

I sniffled.

Shit.

"I'm fine," I said, and rubbed under my nose with the back of my hand.

"Use a tissue, you knacker," Keela said, revolt pulsing through her tone.

I laughed and cried at the same time.

"Leave her alone, Keela." Kane clicked his tongue.

She paid him no attention.

"If you wipe snot onto this blanket so help me God, I'll kill you, Ado."

I continued to laugh, only stopping when I got a stitch in my side.

"Why do you make her laugh like that?" Kane grumbled. "She'll end up hurting herself."

I practically felt Keela roll her eyes.

"Give over, big man. She is pregnant, not made of glass. Give her a bump, I promise she won't break."

Kane grinned wickedly. "Giving her a *bump* is what has me worried about her in the first place."

Keela's eyes shone with wonder. "I can't wait to see what you're like when she gets here; you'll have the poor kid wrapped up in bubble wrap from day one."

"*He* will be a super baby, the chosen one if you will. He won't be fragile."

Keela gleefully laughed. "Keep tellin' yourself that, mate."

I looked up in time to catch Kane stick his middle finger up at Keela and for her to stick up both of hers back at him.

I shook my head good-naturedly.

"Enough, children. Mother is too tired and hungry for your bullshit today," I declared, yawning.

Kane crossed the room and hunkered down next to me. He placed his elbow on the arm of the sofa behind me and gently scratched my back which his fingers. "Why don't you come to bed?"

His voice was low and inviting.

"Maybe because she has company, i.e. me, you dirty bastard." Keela flared. "Stop seducin' her when I'm sittin' right next to your nasty arse."

I beamed at Keela, and Kane smiled at me. He used his free hand to swipe away the already forgotten tears on my cheeks. "There's my babydoll."

Keela giggled. "That's adorable, but you're still nasty."

I flicked my eyes in her direction and playfully narrowed them. "Do you mind?"

"Not at all," she acknowledged. "You do your thing."

Kane nudged me and gave me a wink. "You shouldn't have ever fed her, she'll never leave now."

Keela gasped in mock horror. "I'm not a dog. How dare you!"

"I never said you were." Kane deviously grinned then stood up to his full height. He turned and walked out of our sitting room and headed down the hallway to the kitchen.

Keela pushed my legs, and the blanket that was covering her, off her body and shot to her feet.

"Don't walk away when I'm talkin' to you, Kane Slater!" she hollered, and stomped out of the room after him.

Kane's low laughter did nothing but infuriate her further.

"Or what? You'll kill me?" he teased.

"You're damn right I'll kill you ... don't smile at me like that, I will!"

I chuckled to myself.

They behaved like brother and sister, and I loved it because they loved each other. It would suck balls if my boyfriend and best friend didn't get along.

"Do *not* throw that at me!" Kane's voice suddenly shouted.

Keela cackled. "It's just a tub of butter, you big baby."

"It's a *frozen* tub of butter, so you might as well throw a brick at my head!"

"That can be arranged, big man."

"You're an evil little person, I hope you know that."

"I do."

I laughed at their conversation and sunk back into my sofa, tugging my blanket farther up my body.

"Leave him alone, Keela."

I heard something being set down on either the kitchen counter or table. It dropped with a thud. "You're *lucky* she wants you alive and unharmed."

"And *you're* lucky she wants you here often, otherwise I'd ban you from ever entering this building."

Keela seethed. "You've gone mad with power."

I smiled.

Kane recently told Keela that he owned the building I lived in, as well as many others in Dublin. She wasn't mad, just a little hurt that Alec didn't tell her about Kane's secret properties, but once she got over the 'bro code', she was cool with it like I knew she would be.

She also kept it under wraps, because Kane didn't want it broadcasted to the rest of the group. He liked his privacy and she respected that.

"You better thank God that I have to go home and feed Storm. I'd wipe the floor with you otherwise."

"Till next time, short-ass."

Keela casually strolled into the sitting room and stated, "I hate your boyfriend."

I grabbed my chest. "That's a shame, because I love yours."

Keela's lip twitched. "I'll be back over tonight, I just have to go and feed—"

"The fat beast, I heard you."

Keela growled. "You'd think being pregnant would make you sentimental and give Storm a chance, but no, you *still* rag on him."

In Keela's mind, Storm was her baby.

"He'd make a saint curse, Kay."

Her left eye twitched just before she turned and walked out of my house, giving me the finger along the way. "I'll remember all of this when you're in the height of pain in labour."

I grunted when the apartment door shut. I cringed then and silently prayed karma wouldn't make my labour extra painful, because I teased Storm a lot ... he brought it upon himself most of the time, so when you think about it, I shouldn't suffer because of it.

I leaned back and closed my eyes on a sigh, but just as quickly I snapped them back open. I shot upright when I realised no one was in the room with me.

I was on my own.

Panic struck.

"Kane!" I called out as I looked around the sitting room, expecting someone to jump out and grab me.

I heard his footsteps as he walked down the hallway and into the sitting room, a white mug in his hand with steam rising from it. He quickly sat the mug down on our coffee table when he saw my face and rushed over to me.

"What is it?" he asked and placed a hand on my stomach in silent question.

I swallowed and shook my head. "Nothin', it's just ... I thought I was on my own for a second and... you know, I got scared."

Kane blinked. "You told me you weren't afraid to be on your own anymore."

I looked down. "I lied."

Kane sighed and kneeled on the floor. "I'll kill him for putting such fear into you."

I squeezed my eyes shut as Big Phil's face cut through my mind. "I know."

Kane kissed the side of my head. "Do you want to help me with my injection?"

He could do them himself now, but I appreciated him putting my focus on him instead of the monster that haunted me.

I didn't dream of that night I was trapped in my old classroom, nor did Big Phil's face cut into my dreams. He only plagued me during waking hours when I could sit and think of the 'what ifs'.

What if I didn't get out in time?

What if I inhaled more smoke?

What if he was still close by and watching us, waiting for the right moment to strike?

I didn't voice my thoughts, but they troubled me, and I knew the same questions haunted Kane. He was just keeping it to himself like I was because he didn't want to upset me.

We both suffered in silence.

I knew Kane, his brothers, my brothers, and Keela's uncle Brandon were looking for Big Phil, but none of that eased my mind. He got me once before, and he could do it again if he wanted to. He was that kind of person ... if he wanted something, he got it.

Period.

I think Kane knew that as well. It was one of the reasons I was never without male companionship. When Kane wasn't with me, one of his or my brothers were. It was a round-the-clock security gridlock the lads had going. Kane went as far as to completely seal off the apartment complex I lived in, and he tripled the security detail.

I found none of it comforting though.

My mind was my own worst enemy when it came to running plausible outcomes of Big Phil finding me first before the lads found him. It worried me sick.

"Stop thinking of him."

I looked into Kane's eyes when he spoke and I nodded my head. "I'm tryin', I really am. I just can't help it."

"I will protect you." Kane swore, his eyes locked on mine. "No one will ever hurt you."

I lightly smiled. "Me knight in shinin'... tattoos."

Kane pumped his eyebrows. "I'm adding to my collection soon."

I blinked. "Where about and what are you gettin'?"

He showed me both of his wrists so I reached out and rubbed my thumbs over the small patches of un-inked skin.

"I'm getting your name on my left wrist and our child's on my right wrist. Wrists are a lethal part of the body to be cut; any laceration could potentially be fatal. Without you and our baby I might as well be dead, so I'm putting you both in plain view so I never lose sight of that."

I touched my chest as a lump formed in my throat.

"That was oddly disturbin' and insanely beautiful at the same time."

Kane smirked and my eyes followed the thick scar that curved around his mouth. I stared a little longer than deemed polite, but I couldn't help it. My gaze locked on the marred flesh until my eyes raked over his stunning face and to his arms where more of the thick lumps of damaged tissue lingered.

I loved my man, but I hated that his perfect body was tainted with such marks that brought bulk loads of nasty memories. Lately, I found myself thinking of Big Phil when I focused on Kane's scars for too long. I remembered everything I was told about him, and I didn't think I would ever forget even if I tried. The sick son of a bitch used Kane's vow to protect Damien from harm to his advantage.

Marco Miles was the main man who called the shots over the brothers, but Big Phil held the leash that controlled Kane. He decided how much free-reign he got, and he was the one to viciously jerk on the leash when Kane didn't do as he was told.

That usually happened when Kane refused to hurt innocents. He was strung up with rope by the wrists and received lash upon lash to his body, or he was stabbed with needles as punishment for his defiance. Big Phil found pleasure in torturing and training Kane.

He found pleasure in hurting him.

Kane took his perverted son's life, and in return he wanted my life and our unborn child's. I was terrified of the lengths he would go to seek his vengeance, and I knew that eventually we were all going to clash.

I just didn't know who would be left breathing in the end.

"Babe." Kane's voice jarred me from my thoughts. "Are you okay?"

I blinked my eyes, and looked down to his wrists and lightly smiled.

"I can't wait to see them both when you get them done."

Kane playfully nudged me. "I could get them done tomorrow if junior here would hurry up and vacate your premises."

I giggled. "She will come out when she is good and ready."

"Like a typical woman then?" Kane mused. "Her way or the highway option."

I bobbed my head up and down. "You got it."

"Good thing it's a boy then." He grinned as he leaned in and kissed my head. "I love you, babydoll."

"And I love you."

Kane smiled and said, "You want to know something funny?"

"Always."

"There are over seven billion people on this planet, and I can only tolerate eleven."

I raised an eyebrow. "Who are the eleven people?"

He held up both of his hands and dropped a finger for each person he named. "You, Branna, Bronagh, Keela, Alannah, Alec, Dominic, Ryder, Damien, Tony the pizza delivery guy, and Susan who works in Subway in the village."

I resisted the urge to laugh.

"Why the last two? You don't know them."

Kane pointed his index finger at me. "Tony brings me food, and Susan makes me food. Leave them alone, they're good people."

I snorted. "You really need to expand your circle of people."

"I need to do a lot of things, but that doesn't mean I'm going to." He shrugged.

I grinned. "Why was there no mention of my father or brothers on that list?"

Kane gnawed on his lower lip then smiled wide. "Your family are my ultimate favourites, they're above any list... *obviously*."

I hummed. "Obviously."

"Have I pleased my lady with my answer?" he asked in an awful British accent.

I was about to say yes, when his eyes dropped to my breasts, and he licked his lips.

I playfully rolled my eyes. "You're such a man."

He stood up, took a giant step backwards as his eyes dropped down to his crotch before he looked back to me and said, "I'm aware of that."

"No, like, you're so—"

"Handsome? Sexy? The best sex of your life?"

I narrowed my eyes. "Irritatin'."

"But still handsome, sexy and the best sex of your life?"

My lip twitched. "I suppose."

"I can live with being irritatin' if I've got the rest going for me."

"You're really annoyin' me."

He grinned. "Not irritatin' you?"

"It's the same thing."

"Not really. They're different words."

I was losing my patience.

"They have similar meanin's though," I stated.

Kane folded his arms across his chest. "But they're still different words."

That was it.

"Come closer to me so I can smack you."

"Yeah," he snickered. "Like *that* is going to happen."

I leaned back and closed my eyes. "You drive me crazy, you know that?"

A hand gripped my thigh causing me to jump. I opened my eyes and was surprised to see Kane looming over me. The man could move fast for such a big lad.

"It's only fair since you drive my body crazy all the time."

I waggled my eyebrows. "I wonder if you'll still be lookin' for some when we're in our eighties."

"No doubt about it. I'll speed after you in my wheelchair for some sugar."

I burst into laughter and leaned my head against his when he crawled over me and tucked himself behind me on the sofa.

"How many babies will you give me?" he murmured as his hand absentmindedly stroked my swollen abdomen.

I glanced over my shoulder to him. "How many do you want?"

"At least five."

I gnawed on my lower lip. "Five total or like, five boys? 'Cause we could have all girls, and me body won't be able to go until you get your five aside football team of lads."

Kane rumbled with low laughter. "Five total will be fine. I come from five siblings and you do too. I like the number five."

I leaned back and kissed his forehead. "Five it is, bud."

"They'll have to be close in age, too," he stated. "So right after this one comes out, we'll have to get working on the next one."

My lip curved upward. "So lots and lots of sex then?"

"Yep," he chirped. "We have to make sure your eggo gets preggo."

I laughed and held my stomach.

Kane slid his hand over my hand and gave it a squeeze. "We're having a baby," he whispered.

"We are indeed," I beamed.

"I couldn't be happier, Aideen," Kane said and sat upright. He looked down at me for a long moment before climbing off me and walking out of the room.

I watched him leave the room and confusion caught hold of me. Wanting to know what he was doing, I heaved myself up off the sofa and followed him out of the room, down the hallway and into our bedroom.

"Honey, what's wrong?" I asked from the doorway.

He was standing in front of his nightstand, staring down at something he plucked from the top drawer.

"I wanted to do this after the baby got here, and I wanted it to be perfect and romantic, but I can't wait anymore."

I stared blankly at him as he dropped his hands to his side. He turned to face me then and walked over to me, his eyes locked on mine.

"What are you talkin' about?" I curiously asked.

Kane grabbed my hands gently, took a deep breath, then he did the most out of the blue thing ever.

He got down on one knee.

"Aideen—"

"Omigod." I gasped and pulled my hands from his so I could cover my face.

"I love you more than I ever thought it was possible to love a woman." He smiled wide, his eyes gleaming. "You're my everything, and have completed my life by just existing. I can't put into words the love I'm feeling knowing you're carrying my unborn child... it's mind-blowing. I love you so much, and I was hoping you would do me the honour of becoming my wife."

"Omigod."

With a cheek splitting smile, Kane said the words every girl in her right mind dreamt of hearing, "Will you marry me, babydoll?"

"Kane," I whispered.

Kane lifted his right hand and revealed a large single diamond ring, with mini diamonds filling the band. Without words, I lifted my left hand and watched through blurry eyes as he slid the ring onto my ring finger and then sealed it in place with a forever binding kiss.

"Yes," I said when I found my voice. "Yes, I'll marry you. Yes. Yes. A million times yes!"

Kane sprung to his feet, grabbed my hands and pulled me up against his chest. He crashed his lips to mine and then kissed all over my face as I cried. Tears flowed from my eyes, and hiccups started when I couldn't control the sobs.

"I can't believe this," I wept.

Kane kissed me once more. "I was terrified to ask you in case you said no. I know you love me, but fuck, that was the scariest thing I've ever done. The not knowing took years off my life."

I blinked with shock. "When? How?"

"I bought the ring weeks ago, just after you got... hurt. I then asked your dad and brothers for permission, and after giving me a hard time for a few hours, they gave me their approval and called me an asshole."

I cried again. "You a-asked for per-permission?"

"Of course," Kane responded. "You're precious to your guys, and I wouldn't take you away from them without the go-ahead. I also wouldn't have made it two days before they hunted me down and kicked my ass if I didn't ask."

I laughed as I cried.

I threw my arms around him as best as I could with my stomach keeping me from fully pressing against him. His arms wrapped tightly around me, and for a few seconds we were silent as we held one another. Kane broke the silence when he chuckled.

"What's so funny?" I asked.

Kane pulled back and said, "Damien was just getting used to seeing me with you, and knowing you're really having my kid. Knowing we're engaged will blow his mind."

I beamed as I thought of my new favourite person.

"He will be happy for us," I said with a nod. "They all will be."

Kane pressed his forehead against mine and said, "You're mine forever, now."

I smiled wider than ever before. "I wouldn't have it any other way."

We both turned our heads when a voice shouted, "The favourite brother has arrived!"

I grinned. "Speak of the Devil."

Kane's mouth curved as he took me by the hand and led me out of our bedroom, down the hallway, and into our sitting room where we found Damien setting up Kane's Xbox with two wireless controllers.

"What game do you have?" Kane questioned as he walked over

and dropped onto our sofa.

Damien almost squealed with excitement. "Fifa 16."

Kane clapped his hands together, but stopped when he found me staring. I grinned when he cleared his throat and focused on his brother.

"Heya, Dame."

Damien looked over his shoulder to me and winked, "Hey beautiful."

Kane rolled his eyes, but said nothing as I smiled at his baby brother. He fully accepted that I was head over heels for his brother, just like I was for the rest of the Slater brothers.

"Dame," I whispered.

He looked back to me and smiled as I wiggled the fingers on my left hand at him. He shook his head for a few seconds, not understanding what I was up to until he saw the ring. His brow furrowed together and his lips parted.

He jumped up and spun around to look between Kane and myself with his mouth hanging open.

"Shut the fuck up!" he shouted after a long stretch of silence

Kane burst into laughter, and so did I.

"You *guys*! Is this for real?"

I bobbed my head up and down, my smile stretching from ear to ear. "We're engaged. He just asked me before you walked in. I obviously said hell yes."

Damien's shock was evident, but so was his happiness for us.

"Congratulations," he choked out before rushing forward and wrapping his large arms around me, squeezing me tightly.

When he released me, he dove for Kane. He cursed him out as he began hitting and kicking him as he lay in a mess on the sofa in laughter.

"Three of my brothers are engaged, there is just Dominic left to ask Bronagh," Damien said when he got to his feet.

I smiled. "It'll happen."

"I thought it would have happened when we were teenagers, but

I can feel him doing it soon. He worships the ground that girl walks on."

I hugged my fingered ring to my chest and looked at Kane. "As soon as the girls get here, I'm startin' to plan our weddin'."

Kane swallowed. "Do I need to be heavily involved? I mean, you know I'll do anything and I *want* to be involved, I just don't understand the importance of flowers and colours and such. I don't want to do or say the wrong thing."

I snorted. "Honey, you just need to show up and say I do."

He snapped his fingers at me. "That I can do, babydoll. Deal!"

I grinned and walked out of the room towards the bathroom so I could shower. As I undressed, turned the shower on and waited for the water to heat up, I let my mind drift.

It was hard to believe that Damien was home only six weeks. Even if I tried, I don't think I could ever forget the day when he walked back into his brothers' lives, and dived right into my heart.

He made one hell of an entrance.

Six weeks ago...

"Oh, my God," Kane breathed in disbelief. "Oh, my *fucking* God."

I was right there with him, I couldn't believe who I was seeing.

I reached for Kane, but instead of a hard body, my fingers grasped at thin air. One second Kane was beside my bed, and the next he was across the room lifting his little brother into the air, which wasn't an easy task because Damien was like Nico, he was massive in stature.

"Nice to see you, too." Damien laughed when Kane set him back on the ground.

Kane held him out at arm's length, stared at him for another long moment then crushed him with another hug.

Damien wheezed and slapped at Kane's sides. "Can't... breathe."

I laughed, but winced in pain.

My throat hurt so badly.

"Damien!" Kane repeated out loud and touched his face like he was trying to check if he was real. "Fuck. Little brother, you're here."

Damien beamed and nodded. "I'm here."

Kane shook his head in disbelief. "How are you here? I mean, I'm not complaining, I just don't understand what is going on right now."

"Dominic called me last night and told me what happened. I got on the first flight out. I landed about an hour ago and came straight here."

Kane rubbed his face with his hands. "The others don't know you're here?"

Damien shook his head. "No, I didn't tell Dominic in case I couldn't get a flight."

Kane exhaled a big breath. "Shit. He'll kill you for not telling him."

Damien guffawed. "I know."

Without warning, Kane hugged Damien again. "I just can't believe you're really here. I'm tripping hard on this."

Damien patted Kane's back, but said nothing as they shared a special moment. When they pulled apart, Kane turned and with a bright smile on his face, he gestured to me.

"This is Aideen, my lady," he moved closer to me and rubbed my stomach, "and this is baby Slater, your niece or nephew."

Damien stared at my stomach. "I still can't believe that. It's insane to think you're going to be a daddy."

"Tell me about it."

Damien flicked his big grey eyes up from my belly and his gaze focused on my face. He stepped up beside Kane and looked down at me and purred. "Hello, gorgeous. It's a *privilege* to finally meet your fine self in person."

Oh, the kid oozed charm.

God help the girl he set his sights on, the lass didn't have a chance.

Kane side-eyed his brother then, out of nowhere, he lifted his hand and whacked him across the back of the head.

"Damn it," Damien rumbled with laughter and rubbed the back

of his head. "My reflexes aren't what they used to be. I knew that was coming, but I still couldn't move to stop it."

Kane smiled with glee. "You'll learn."

Damien shook his head, smiling, then he looked back at me. I was staring at him with non-blinking eyes and he found it amusing.

"I know, you're wondering why you're with this doofus," he jabbed his thumb at Kane, "when you could have had all of this." He gestured to his body and did a little hip wiggle.

I wanted to laugh, but the best I could do was make a gurgle sound that still hurt and caused me to wince in pain.

"Dame," Kane chastised with a concerned frown. "Don't make her laugh; her throat is pretty torn up. She inhaled a lot of smoke and choked on it so much that she has gashes and cuts from all the coughing."

Damien's face fell. "I'm so sorry, Aideen. I didn't know."

I waved Kane off and gave Damien a tight-lipped smile. I proceeded to silently study him. I hoped he couldn't tell, but I was so freaked out. I had never met identical twins in real life, and the likeness between Damien and Nico was uncanny.

"If your hair was brown," I whispered and withheld a wince. "I'd think you were Nico."

"Good thing my hair is blond then," Damien winked.

He even sounded like Nico, which made the entire experience stranger for me.

Kane snickered at me. "Why are you looking at him like that?"

Like what?

I shrugged my shoulders without looking away from Damien. "I'm tryin' to find somethin' else to separate him from Nico... I'm freaked out here. There are *two* of them." My voice was so low; I saw the brothers strain to hear what I said.

I always knew they were twins, but seeing Damien in person really messed with my mind because he looked so much like Nico that it was scary. I've heard the girls list the differences between them, but for the life of me I couldn't spot one besides hair colour.

Damien laughed at my bugged out expression. "This is cool. I haven't been around someone being weirded out by me and Dominic in a long time."

Kane patted his brother's back. "You're home now, you have plenty of time for all that again."

Damien nodded. "It feels good to be back."

"It feels even better to have you back," Kane said cheerfully. "You'll be here for my baby being born, bro. You've no idea how happy that makes me."

Damien's teeth gleamed like pearls when he smiled. "I'm still tripping that you're going to be a dad, *and* that I'm going to be an uncle."

Kane looked at my bump. "I think I'll be tripping on it until he is grown."

"She," I whispered absentmindedly.

Damien looked between both Kane and myself. "Do either of you know the gender?"

"Technically *no*," Kane chortled, "but I think it's a boy and Aideen thinks it's a girl."

Damien raised his hand. "I'm team boy. We know how to handle Slater men. Slater women on the other hand? We have zero experience on that front."

"Amen to that," Kane breathed. "Can you imagine little Irish versions of Slater women? Fuck, too terrifying to even think about."

I devilishly grinned as I whispered, "They'll look and talk like us girls, I don't see the problem."

Kane deadpanned, "You wouldn't because *you're* the woman."

I laughed a little, but quickly reached for my throat with my good hand.

Kane placed his hand on my arm. "No more talking, okay?"

I nodded to Kane and looked back to Damien and continued to stare at him.

He cracked under my gaze after a full minute.

"Stop staring at me, I feel like I'm being violated!"

Kane laughed at that then retook his seat at the head of my bed. "How did you know she was in this hospital?"

Damien sat on the end of my bed. "Dominic mentioned it during his phone call last night and I got the first flight out."

Kane scratched the stubble on his chin. "I thought you were saving your money and staying for your Christmas bonus?"

Damien furrowed his eyebrows together. "My future sister-in-law is seriously injured and you expected me to stay put over three thousand miles away? Get the fuck outta here."

I smiled and Kane snickered. "My bad, I should have known better."

"Yeah," Damien agreed. "You should have."

I watched the pair of them talk. They teased each other, hit each other, hugged each other and just enjoyed being in each other's company.

It was beautiful.

I closed my eyes and started to drift off, but when Kane spoke next, sleeping was out of the question.

"What are you going to do about Alannah?" Kane suddenly asked Damien.

My interest peaked.

I cracked my eyes open, but quickly closed them again when Damien glanced in my direction. "Inside voice, bro."

"It's fine, she's sleeping," Kane replied.

Damien scratched his neck and quietly he said, "I'm going to pray she doesn't gut me when she sees me."

Kane lightly chortled. "She's not Bronagh, she won't hurt you."

"You say that now," Damien grumbled, "but you don't know how much she hates me."

"No," Kane chuckled. "I'm serious. She won't hurt you. The girl is the polar opposite to the rest of them, she wouldn't hurt a fly. She doesn't even raise her voice that much... how she is Bronagh's best friend still baffles me. They're so different."

Opposites attract, even in friends.

"Do you guys spend a lot of time with her?" Damien asked Kane since I was still pretending to be sleeping.

"Yeah, she's part of the girl's little clique. When she's not working, or with her parents, she is hanging with us." I could hear the smile in Kane's voice as he spoke. "The girl is killer sweet, bro. She's adorable."

Damien's swallow was audible.

"I'm nervous as hell to see her. What if she blows up at me?" he questioned.

"What if she is completely okay and greets you like a normal human being? That shit between you both happened years ago, she's probably forgotten about it."

Was Kane not in the room months ago when Alannah left the house when Damien was on a FaceTime call in her presence? That girl hasn't forgotten a damn thing.

"Maybe," Damien mumbled. "Coming back here has me all kinds of messed up. Not in a bad way, so you can stop frowning at me, I just mean it's so surreal. It feels like I never left."

"You'll want to leave after a week in our house. It's never empty, and the girls are so loud."

Cheeky pig!

"Worse than just Bronagh and Branna?" Damien chuckled.

"Way worse. Keela and Aideen are like their hype girls, they make them even louder."

Damien laughed. "I can't believe the four of you are in steady relationships. I'm the only single one. How fucked up is that? You all used to be scared of the word 'girlfriend'."

Kane snorted. "I'm *still* scared of it, scared of her, but just of how much I love her. It's terrifying to me that something could happen to her and she wouldn't be here anymore. I almost lost her last night, bro. I'd cease to exist if I didn't have her, and I've no doubt that feeling will triple when she has the baby."

I heard a patting sound. "We'll protect her, and the baby."

"We have to, they're both my life."

"She's a Slater, we take care of our own."

I heard the pride in Kane's voice when he said, "Yeah, I guess she is a Slater."

"She is, and so are the other three. Bronagh, Branna, Keela and Aideen are it for you guys, I can tell just by the way you all talk about them."

Kane sighed. "Ryder and Branna are struggling."

Silence.

"Dominic mentioned he was worried about them," Damien murmured.

"It's bad, and I don't think they're going to come out of it still together." He lowered his voice more. "Don't say that to any of the girls, God only knows what they will do if they knew Ryder and Branna might break up for real."

I inwardly rolled my eyes.

We weren't stupid, we knew things with Ryder and Branna weren't good. We were just more optimistic than the lads that they would work it out. I had faith in the pair of them. Everyone has their bad patches, and this was Ryder and Branna's.

I opened my eyes and moved when I heard a voice outside the door of my room. It sounded similar to Damien, which meant it was Nico.

"That's Nico," I rasped.

Kane looked at me with surprised eyes before he switched his attention to Damien and jerked his head in the direction of the door. Without speaking a word, Damien leaped to his feet and shot over to the door and hid behind it.

Kane rubbed his hands together and looked to me. "Ten euros he cries."

I snorted, but didn't take the bet.

Kane and I looked to the door when Nico stepped into the room, pocketing his phone.

"Hey," he smiled at me as he slapped hands with his brother. "I thought you'd be sleeping."

"I'll sleep later," I whispered.

A shadow moved behind Nico, and with a hidden smile, I watched as Damien crept up behind his brother.

"Are you feeling better?" Nico asked me, his eyes filled with concern.

"Of course she is," Damien responded. "She finally saw my face in person, and that makes everything better."

Nico swung around so fast he almost tripped himself up.

"Damien!" he roared. "What the fuck?"

Like lightening Nico sprung forward, and dove onto Damien who was laughing as he opened his arms wide. Nico's chest collided with Damien's and his arms wrapped around his twin while his face dropped to Damien's shoulder.

Damien was smiling as he clapped his hands against Nico's back, but he soon lowered his head to Nico's shoulder and they let their emotions out.

I let my emotions out too; I was in tears watching them.

"You're both making Aideen cry, you assholes."

Both Nico and Damien laughed as they separated and wiped their eyes discreetly. They only parted for a second though, because they quickly hugged again. They patted each other on the back a lot and called each other crude names.

"You fucking dick," Nico stated and punched Damien in the shoulder. "Why didn't you tell me you were coming home? I was not prepared, bro, not prepared at all. You just made me fucking cry!"

Damien laughed and wiped under both of his eyes. "What? You're too cool to cry?"

"I don't cry!" Nico growled, brushing the back of his right hand across his cheeks.

I grunted. "You cried when Kane was in hospital and we found out he was going to be okay."

Kane perked up. "Aww, sweet little brother, you *do* care."

"Fuck you, Kane!" Nico snapped then flicked his eyes to me.

"Couldn't have kept that to yourself, could you, princess?"

I grinned. "No, *husband*."

Nico's lip quirked.

"What does she mean by husband?" Damien questioned, his eyebrow raised.

"Yeah," Kane chimed in, his brows drawn together. "What the fuck does she mean by husband?"

Nico chortled. "The day you collapsed I had to pretend to the security guard in the ER that Bronagh, Branna, Aideen and Alannah were all my wives. He said they needed to be family so I said they were. He believed me, too," he said proudly.

Kane waited only a second before he burst into laughter. Damien and Nico quickly followed suit.

I rolled my eyes.

Brothers.

"Worst day ever," I whispered.

That shut them up.

Kane leaned over to me and kissed my head. "I think the worst day ever occurred last night, babydoll."

When I got hurt.

I blinked. "Do you think he knows I didn't die?"

The brothers' faces hardened. Any mention of Big Phil, or their old life, seemed to have that effect on them.

"Wait till I find that motherfucker," Nico grumbled under his breath.

"Not here," Kane muttered to his brother then focused on me. "Don't think about him, he doesn't deserve a second of your time. Think about our little one. It's not long now until he is here."

I didn't think I would ever stop thinking about the man who almost killed my unborn child, an innocent student, as well as me.

I thought of Caleb then, and felt so grateful to him. Most teenage boys wouldn't have risked getting hurt in order to help a teacher of theirs, but Caleb did. I met his parents earlier in the day and thanked them profusely for their son's bravery. I didn't get a chance to talk to him, because like me, his throat was pretty torn up from coughing. The good news was he would be leaving the hospital soon, which comforted me; it meant he wasn't harmed as badly as he could have been.

I smiled for Kane's sake and said, "She."

Kane grinned. "You aren't going to let up on that, are you?"

"Nope, because she is a girl," I whispered.

"You're going to give my son a complex, calling him a girl all the time."

I smiled wide and rested my head back against my pillow.

"Where is Bee?" Damien asked Nico as the three of them sat down.

Damien sat back down on the end of my bed, but was mindful that he didn't touch my injured leg. You couldn't miss it though even if you tried. The cast on it was bright blue, and there was a ramp of sorts along with pillows tucked under it to keep it elevated.

Nico jabbed his thumb over his shoulder. "She was following me up. She wanted to park my car."

"And you let her?" Damien gasped.

Nico laughed. "I taught her how to drive, she's decent."

The *'for a girl'* he implied in that statement was silent.

"I want to freak her out," Damien stated happily. "How will I do that?"

Nico stood up and shrugged out of his grey hoodie. "Put this on and sit with your back to the door. There are no extra seats so she will sit on your lap thinking you're me."

Oh, this was going to be so good.

Damien had a shit-eating grin on his face as he put Nico's hoodie over his head. Nico moved over to the door and hid in the same spot Damien did only minutes before. Damien then sat in Nico's seat and pulled up the hood as Kane fluffed up the blanket on the bed, making it look like there was less room to sit down than there really was.

We waited a few minutes, but when the door to my room

opened, we all held our breath.

"Hey," Bronagh whispered as she stepped into the room and closed the door behind her without turning around.

"She's awake," Kane smiled. "No need to whisper."

"Oh," Bronagh frowned and walked over. "Have you slept much?"

I shook my head.

"How are you feelin'?" she asked as her eyes scanned the room for a seat. When she saw there was none, she did exactly what Nico said she would do. She touched Damien's shoulder and she moved around him and sat on his lap. Damien's arms went around her, snuggling against her.

"I'm much better," I whispered, smiling.

Bronagh's eyes brightened. "I'm so happy to hear that, after last nice that's so good to hear. You're on the mend."

I nodded my head and just stared at her.

She was unknowingly resting against Damien's chest. She glanced at Kane and myself and furrowed her eyes when she found us staring. She leaned her head back to speak to who she thought was Nico, but as soon as her eyes landed on Damien's face, she instantly widened them.

"Damien!" she screamed and wrapped herself around him.

I threw my uninjured arm up in the air.

"How can she tell?" I rasped and tucked my burned forearm against my chest. "I want to know the difference between them, I don't like not knowin'."

Kane was laughing at me, and so was Nico who came out of the corner of the room. He lost his smile as he walked over and kicked his brother's leg when Damien's hand slipped very low on Bronagh's back.

"Oh, give me a break," Damien groaned. "I haven't touched her in *years*!"

"I love you, but I'll break all your fingers if you don't let go of her."

Damien removed his hands from Bronagh and held them up in the air. Snickering he said, "She's the one who is all over me, bro."

"Damn it, Bronagh," Nico snapped, but he had a smile on his face as he said it.

"I'm not lettin' go," Bronagh cried. "He might run away again."

Damien rolled his eyes. "I'm not going anywhere you big baby."

"Speaking of a *baby*," Kane grinned.

Nico looked to Kane and smiled before he looked to Damien. Damien looked to Nico and frowned. "Whose baby? Kane's?"

Nico shook his head.

"Then whose?"

Nico nodded at Bronagh, and Damien moved his line of sight to the blubbering mess on his lap. For a second Damien stared down at her, then his eyes bugged out.

"*Bronagh's* pregnant?!"

Nico joyfully laughed. "Yeah, bro."

"Oh, my God!" Damien shouted at his brother in shock. "Dominic, shut the *fuck* up!"

Everyone burst into laughter. I almost did, but I quickly stopped myself before I slipped up. I really sucked at not speaking or making noise.

"You're *really* pregnant?" Damien asked Bronagh, his smile almost touching his ears.

Bronagh nodded her head, her eyes shining with tears. "I'm *really* pregnant."

"Congratulations!" He beamed and kissed her face then hugged her tightly before standing up with Bronagh still in his arms and crushing her into a hug with Nico. Nico laughed and hugged the both of them, happiness radiating from him.

"Is anyone else pregnant?" he questioned. "Tell me now because my heart can't deal with all of this excitement."

Bronagh laughed and hugged Damien tightly. "It's just me and Aideen so far."

"Holy. Fuck."

He punched Nico then and said, "You aren't shooting blanks after all."

"Ha ha ha," Nico said, but grinned like a fool.

"Why didn't you tell me you cocksucker?" Damien asked Nico, a frown forming on his beautiful face.

Nico held up his hands. "She just told me last night. I was in the dark for awhile too, bro."

We all looked at Bronagh when she nudged between Damien and Nico, and wrapped her arms back around Damien. "I missed you so much."

He held her and kissed the crown of her head. "I missed you too, babe."

I watched them with a huge smile on my face and said, "Where are the others? I want to see them surprised, too. It's so much fun."

Everyone laughed.

"I'll call them and tell 'em to come by," Kane said and took out his phone.

Nico curiously asked, "What will you tell them?"

"That there is good news and I want all the family here before I tell them what it is. It'll get them here."

I grinned.

It'd get them here alright.

We spent the next thirty minutes talking, sharing old and new stories with Damien when Kane suddenly hushed up and jumped to his feet. He shot to the door and cracked it open before quickly closing it.

"They're coming," he rushed. "Dame, behind the door. Quickly."

Damien ran for the door and slipped behind it just as the door opened and Alec stepped into the room. He paused when he saw Kane was right next to the door. He stared at him.

"Where are you going?"

"Nowhere," Kane replied. "I heard you guys talking so I was

just getting the door for you all."

"Oh." Alec's features relaxed. "Thanks, bro. That's nice of you."

We breathed a sigh of relief when he entered the room followed by Ryder, Keela and Branna. I smiled when I saw her. She took time off work just so she could go back and forth between the hospital to help Kane and me with whatever we needed over the next few days.

She was a sweetheart, but looked a shell of her former self as she stood next to Ryder.

"What's the news?" she asked. "You said it was good news on the phone to Alec."

"It *is* good news," Kane began, a slow smile stretching across his face. "But it's not something I can show or tell you."

Ryder raised a brow. "Who can then?"

I chuckled as Damien rounded on Keela's right and came up next to Kane, patting his shoulder.

"I'll take it from here, bro."

I smiled wide as realisation washed over Branna, Ryder, Keela and Alec. Branna let her phone and bag drop to the floor as she shot forward.

"Damien!" She cried and jumped into his open arms.

He laughed as he caught her in mid-air and locked his arms tightly around her. "Mama bear, I've missed you."

Branna burst into tears as Damien's brothers and Keela stared at him with wide eyes. Ryder stepped forward and, without hesitation, he grabbed hold of Damien. This resulted in a Slater brother sandwich with a Branna filling.

I momentarily wondered if that was the closest contact both Ryder and Branna had with one another since their problems started. I shook my head clear of that worry and looked to Alec and Keela. Keela was in tears as she hugged a close-to-crying Alec.

"You little bastard," he sniffled. "I'm going to cry."

Damien laughed and stretched his neck so he could see over Ryder and Branna. "Dominic cried, too, if it makes you feel better."

"You asshole!" Nico angrily spat making Damien crack up laughing. "You said you wouldn't tell anyone."

Alec wiped under his eyes. "That does make me feel better, actually."

"My bad, bro," Damien chuckled to Nico.

Nico rolled his eyes, but smiled at his twin. He looked to Bronagh then who was staring at Damien with a cheek-splitting smile.

"Happy, are we?" he murmured and slipped his hand around her waist and tugged her closer to his side.

Her hands instantly went to her abdomen as her head bobbed up and down. She looked at Dominic as her eyes welled with tears. "I'm happier than I've ever been. He's home, and we're goin' to have a baby. A *real* baby, Dominic."

Dominic leaned his head down to Bronagh's and brushed his lips over hers. "The first of many, pretty girl."

"Awwww."

Everyone looked at me, and it caused me to blush. Kane chuckled at me and nudged me to scoot over on my bed so he could climb up and sit next to me.

"I love you," I whispered to him.

He looked me dead in the eye and said, "I love you, too."

"Hell must have frozen over for Kane to be in love," Damien commented, making everyone snicker.

I grinned and nudged Kane's cheek with my nose.

"You mean you didn't see the pigs flying around outside?" I teased.

Damien laughed.

"Dimples!" I rasped. "Nico has dimples and you don't... wait, no, you kind of do. Little ones. Damn it."

Damien focused his devastating smile in my direction.

"Just stick with the hair, beautiful. It's what everyone else does."

I melted. "I'll find something. Eventually. I'll just have to stare at you a lot until I do."

"Fine by me."

"But not by me," Kane growled.

"Please," Nico laughed. "I catch her staring at me all the time. All those crotch stares were wannabe cock stares."

Kane was off the bed and tackling Nico to the floor within seconds. Damien took Kane's spot next to me on my bed and together we watched Nico and Kane go at it in the middle of my hospital room. He laced his hand behind his head and he grinned. "It's so fucking good to be home."

It *was* good. Our family was whole now, and growing.

With his brothers was where Damien belonged.

I leaned my head on his shoulder and smiled.

Who would have thought I'd be falling in brotherly love with another Slater brother?

Not me, that was for damn sure.

CHAPTER THREE

"Aideen?"

I shook my head and pulled my thoughts from Damien's homecoming and popped my head out of the shower when I heard Kane's voice.

"I'm in the shower. Is everythin' okay?"

"Yeah, I just wanted to see how long you will be? I wanna shower too."

I wasn't even in the shower that long.

"I don't know," I replied. "I'm trying to wash my legs, but it's hard to bend."

The bathroom door opened, and in stepped Kane in just his boxer shorts.

Fuck.

I let my eyes trail down his body, and bite my lower lip at the sight.

"You're lucky you're already pregnant," he growled, watching my eyes admire him.

I flicked my gleaming eyes to him and grinned. "You joinin' me?"

He nodded so I stepped back into the shower to make room for him. I turned to put my pouf down but jumped and let it fall from my fingertips when I felt Kane's hard body press up against me. His strong hands flattened against my belly and turned me to face him as they slid around and down to my behind.

I stood up straight and gave Kane a knowing look. "Don't play, you don't want to get me worked up today. I'd eat you up."

Kane smirked. "Is that a challenge?"

I closed my eyes when his head dipped, and his lips came into contact with my neck. I groaned in response and Kane gave my behind another squeeze before bringing his hand up to my waist.

"You're so warm," he murmured against my skin.

I smiled and opened my eyes. "Are you callin' me hot?"

"*Smoking* hot."

I giggled and looked down. "Can you get me the pouf, it fell."

Kane bent, grabbed the luffa, kissed my belly then stood up and towered over me.

I gazed up at him. "I love that you're taller than me."

"It doesn't hurt your neck looking up at me?" he questioned.

I wickedly grinned. "You usually get me on my back before I get a chance to feel any kind of strain."

Kane laughed as he stuck his head under the spray of hot water, soaking his hair and face with the droplets. I squeezed some liquid body wash onto my pouf and continued my job of scrubbing myself. Kane took it from me when I was done; he bent down and rubbed it over my legs and behind, cleansing my skin.

"Open your legs for me," he asked, his voice gruff.

I did as requested as he lathered his hand in body wash. I licked my lips when his hands rubbed up and down my inner thighs before cupping my pussy. I reached down and fisted my hand in his hair when his fingers moved closer to my clit and began to swirl around the sensitive bundle of nerves.

"*Oh.*"

I felt Kane move his body, but was glad he kept his hand between my thighs. His teeth suddenly nipped my nipple and it caused me to open my eyes and hiss at him.

"Sensitive."

He smiled coyly at me before putting his mouth on me, rubbing his lips gently over the now hardened peak. My breathing turned rapid as the sensation quickly flooded my body. I felt Kane's free arm wind around my waist as he picked up the pace with his fingers.

"Come on, baby," he whispered when he detached his mouth from my nipple and moved it to my ear.

"I—*ah*."

He stuck his tongue in my ear and it caused my eyes to roll back just as my core exploded. I think I screamed when he pinched my pulsing clit only to massage it once more causing my hips to buck into his hand as I rode out my orgasm.

Time silently passed by as I came back down to Earth, and when I opened my eyes I found my stunning boyfriend looming over me with a smug expression on his face.

"Ninety seconds."

I lazily smiled at him. "It happens so fast because I'm sensitive, you know that. I will go back to normal after the baby is born."

His smug-as-fuck grin deepened. "I got you off in less than two minutes the night I knocked you up."

I raised my eyebrow. "You counted the seconds it took for me to come?"

"Of course."

I guffawed. "Is that a lad thing?"

Kane shrugged. "Probably just a me thing."

I leered at him for a few moments before bowing my head and pressing it against his hard chest. Seconds passed by when I suddenly shivered. Kane felt my shiver and turned us so my back was directly under the hot spray of the showerhead.

I hummed. "That is *so* nice."

"Is your back still sore?" he quizzed as he rubbed his hands over my shoulders.

I nodded. "It's just because of all the weight I'm carryin' around my front with the baby."

"How about a massage after we finish showering?"

"Sounds good to me, daddy."

I was about to speak when Kane suddenly said, "Did you just pee?"

I scrunched up my face in disgust. "Ew. No. Why would you ask that?"

"The water got a little warmer all of a sudden."

I frowned. "I didn't wee."

"It's okay if you did—"

"Kane." I cut him off. "I didn't wee."

He grinned teasingly at me. "There are two types of people in the world, those who pee in the shower, and those who lie about it."

I balled my hands into fists.

"I did *not* piss in the bloody shower."

"You're a liar."

"KANE!" I screeched. "I went to the toilet *before* I got in. If I pissed in the fuckin' shower, I'd say it."

"Uh-huh."

"I'll piss on *you* if you keep this up."

"Is that a way of marking your territory?"

I covered my face with my hands.

"I hate you," I grumbled.

"Now I definitely know you're lying."

I lowered my hands and glared at him. "I *do* hate you."

He smiled. "Then I love the way you hate me."

My lip quirked and he saw it.

"Ah-ha! Made you smile, you can't be mad anymore."

I grunted, "How old are you? Fifteen? A smile doesn't get you off the hook, I can mutely be pissed for weeks, even years."

Kane blinked. "Even against your baby daddy?"

"*Especially* against my baby daddy."

Kane's look of horror caused me to laugh. He pulled me close and kissed the crown of my head and helped me finish washing myself in places I couldn't reach. He even washed and conditioned my hair simply because he enjoyed doing it for me.

I did my part and scrubbed his back for him, every so often stopping to kiss one of his many scars which made him smile as he watched me through the reflection of the glass. He kept rubbing the steam away so he could watch what I was doing, and it gave me excited chills knowing he couldn't keep his eyes off me.

We both stayed under the spray of water, just touching and kissing one another until the water began to run cold. We got out then and Kane wrapped me in a huge white towel that I snuggled into. I watched as he wrapped a smaller towel around his lower half.

"I do be freezin' gettin' out of the shower; it's why I snuggle into towels like this. Do you not get cold since you have nothin' coverin' your upper body?"

Kane snickered at my question. "Sometimes I do, sometimes I don't. It never matters because it only takes me a few minutes to dry and put some clothes on."

I exhaled. "I'm not like you at all. I sit on my bed, wrapped in my towel for ages before the urge to get dressed hits."

"Is that a woman thing?" Kane teased, repeating my earlier words.

I chortled. "Probably just a me thing."

"Doubtful," Kane joked. "I can imagine Bronagh doing the same thing as you though she's much lazier than you are."

I took no offence at being called lazy because it was true.

I giggled. "Don't let her hear you say that. She's been doin' so well after finishin' her anger management program, but you *know* her anger is somethin' she has to deal with for life. Don't be the cause of her relapse."

Kane held both of his hands in the air. "Dominic can do that all on his own without my help."

I rubbed water from my nose onto my towel, then I watched as Kane dried his delicious body before he slipped on a pair of skin-tight boxer shorts. I frowned when my eyes landed on his left thigh.

"Switch to your right leg when injectin' your insulin for a while," I mumbled. "Your left one is all bruised up."

Kane looked down to his leg then up to me. "Hey, don't be sad, it's only some bruises. I can't even feel them."

But I can see them.

"I just hate that you have to inject yourself every day for the rest of your life, and balance your diet otherwise bad stuff happens."

Don't think about the bad stuff.

"It's a small price to pay, babydoll. You know it is."

I did, but it still sucked.

"You're doin' okay, aren't you?" I asked with hopeful eyes.

He nodded. "I'm doing awesome, sweetheart."

"You promise?"

"I promise."

That relaxed me.

The last thing I needed was Kane being ill from his diabetes again. The last time that happened it fucking sucked. It also scared me, and everyone else, to death.

"Get dressed."

I blinked at the sudden request. "Why?"

"My brothers are here. The rest of them, I mean."

"Kane," I groused. "You could have told me that. This is so embarrassin'. I could deal with Damien because he has that video game volume on high, but I wouldn't have let you in the shower with me had I known they were *all* here."

Kane smirked at me. "Like you could have stopped me."

"Good point," I grumbled.

Kane stared at me so I sighed and waved him on.

"You go on out to them, I can dress meself. I'm not an invalid."

Kane didn't argue with me. He kissed my head and rushed out of the room, closing the door behind him. No doubt he wanted to get back to playing that stupid football game.

I took my time drying my hair and my body before dressing myself in leggings, a tank top and one of Kane's hoodies. I slipped my feet into my slippers and tied my hair up in a bun before I exited my room.

I heard Kane and his brothers talking, so naturally I remained quiet to hear what they were saying. I crept closer to the sitting room, paused next to the open door and listened.

"How can you be scared of her? She's tiny with a pregnant belly." Nico belly laughed.

Kane lowered his voice. "I'm not scared of *her*. I'm scared of the *hormones*."

Nico matched his voice to Kane's in volume. "Why are you talking about them like they're a separate being?"

"They *are* a separate being," Kane stated. "They're pure fucking evil. Do you understand me? Evil."

Damien snickered. "Hormones don't go away, you know? Women are always hormonal, it just triples during pregnancy."

"Exactly, I just have to survive the next few weeks, then things will go back to the way they normally were."

Ryder guffawed. "You mean when Aideen spat curse words whenever she saw you?"

"Ahhh," Kane sighed. "The good ol' days."

I covered my mouth so they wouldn't hear me giggle. With a smile, I walked backwards a few steps and that made a little stomp sound which sent the sitting room into dead silence. I wiped the smile off my face as I walked into the room, raising my eyebrows when I found all eyes on me.

"Are you all okay?"

They nodded, but didn't reply to my question.

"Are you *sure*?"

Again, they mutely nodded their heads.

I eyed them and said, "Okaaaay."

I walked over to the sofa and took the free space next to Alec. He absentmindedly put his arm around my shoulders, so I nestled into his side and watched as the others played their football game and chatted amongst themselves.

"Alec," I murmured.

He glanced down at me. "Hmm?"

"Do you still think Matt Bomer is hot?"

He snorted. "Yeah, why?"

I shrugged. "I thought Keela might block out all the good looking dick holders of the world."

Alec burst out into laughter, and even Kane—who was close to us—laughed.

"I'm not blind, darling, just too in love to notice anyone else."

My heart melted.

"You're strictly a female worshipper now?"

"I'm strictly a *Keela* worshipper now."

I smiled. "When did you know you were bi?"

"I've always known."

"Really?"

He nodded.

"I was never straight and I was never gay, I have always been bi-sexual. I just happened to have slept with more men than woman. I mean, it's not like I flipped a switch and decided its dick o'clock for the next six hours then it's pussy time. I liked who I liked, regardless of gender."

Alec's brothers laughed, but I was too into the conversation to crack a smile.

"And now?" I questioned.

"And now I don't see anyone but Keela. No man, no woman, just her."

I beamed. "That's so sweet."

Kane chortled. "Alec isn't sweet."

"I beg to differ," I shot back. "He is very sweet."

Alec pounded his closed fist against his chest. "Don't hate, bro, embrace that your girl thinks I'm so... *sweet*."

Kane tried to get up so he could hit Alec, but I held Kane in place with my legs and sprawled over the sweet human as I stopped the impending fight.

"Leave him be!" I shouted.

"He is referring to something sexual!"

I rolled my eyes. "How do you know that?"

"Because he is my brother and I know him."

I leaned my head back and looked up to Alec. "Are you tryin' to piss him off?"

Alec shrugged, a knowing grin playing on his lips. "I'm bored, baiting him amuses me."

Brothers.

"Don't fight," I groaned and turned into Kane's body. "I'm too pregnant to try to stop it."

Kane placed his hand on my hip. "Why don't you go to bed?"

"Because if I sleep now then I'll be awake all night."

Nico scoffed from across the room. "Go into labour and get the brat out then."

I snickered, "I can't just go into labour. It will happen when it happens. I've two weeks left until me due date anyway, and it's very common to go overdue... up to *two weeks* over, now that I think of it."

"Oh, my God," Alec gasped with a hand placed dramatically over his chest. "We can't wait that long. Eight and a half months is long enough!"

Tell me about it.

"What helps induce labour?" Nico curiously asked.

I shrugged. "Long walks, spicy food, herbal teas, sex—"

"Do that!" Alec cut me off.

I snorted. "I would, but Kane won't have sex with me."

"What?" Alec and Nico asked in unison then looked at their brother with a mixture of shock and disgust.

Ryder and Damien looked at him with disbelieving eyes, too.

"Don't you pricks judge me," Kane snapped and pointed his index finger at them. "You try having sex with your girl when she is close to birthing a child. I'm fucking terrified I'll bump his head or something... he is so low. He has a secure hold of her pussy now. It's literally off limits. I just... I can't touch her like that. That's my kid's *mom!*"

I rolled my eyes having heard this excuse a billion times over the last week and a half.

"Is it weird that I'm picturing what Aideen's pussy looks like now?" Nico muttered aloud.

I gasped. "Yes, you pervert!"

"Don't blame me," Nico stated and looked at Kane, "*he* brought your pussy into it."

The word pussy was starting to sound weird to me.

I held my hands in the air. "Let's just stop talking about me *vagina*, okay? Brilliant."

A veil of silence fell upon the room until Alec opened his mouth.

"I'll do it if Kane won't."

"Bro."

I looked at Alec with a raised eyebrow. "Are you offerin' to have sex with me?"

"Yes," Alec replied without hesitation. "I really want you to have my nephew... I'm willing to do *anything* to help bring on labour."

Was it weird that my first reaction was to defend the gender of my unborn child as female instead of rejecting my boyfriend's brother's offer to bed me?

"Five seconds."

I blinked when Kane's voice got my attention. His body was no longer under my legs. I looked up and found Kane, who was now standing over Alec like an animal ready to attack.

Alec leaned as far back into the sofa as he possibly could. "Bro, I'm trying to help-"

"Three seconds."

"Oh, come on, this is a sweet gesture when you-"

"One second."

Alec jumped to his feet and exited my apartment shouting, "At least think about it," as he ran.

"I've never seen him move so fast in my life." Nico snickered.

"It's like he caught a glimpse of the Magic Mike cast and took off after them."

I burst into unexpected laughter and laughed so hard I thought a little pee came out.

"I. Love. Your. Brothers."

Kane looked from the sitting room door to a laughing Nico, Damien and Ryder and grunted, "I hate the bastards."

CHAPTER FOUR

"**S**hut. Up!" Female voices screamed over one another.

I covered my ears and laughed.

My left hand was snatched away from my ear as Bronagh pulled it up to her face and inspected my *killer* engagement ring.

"It's gorgeous," she gushed.

Keela and Branna huddled closer and gushed over the ring, too.

"How did he ask?" Keela squealed. "And when?"

I had a massive smile on my face as I told them how Kane proposed and what he said and did whilst proposing. Each of the girls clutched their chest and sighed dreamily.

"I love your *fiancé*," Keela giggled, emphasising the word.

I chuckled. "Yeah, he's a bit of all right."

"Is it goin' to be a forever engagement like mine, or a quick one?" Branna asked. Her eyes were on me, but her mind was clearly elsewhere.

I hesitated and said, "Sooner rather than later, I think. He wants to get pregnant again right after the baby is born so all our kids are close in age. I don't want to be whale sized in my dress, so sooner. *Definitely* sooner."

Keela's jaw dropped. "What? How many children does he want?"

"Five," I replied.

Bronagh gasped. "Dominic wants five, too."

I looked between the girls and blinked. "They all want five?"

Keela held up her finger and plucked her phone from her pocket, tapped the screen, put the phone on speaker and held it face up in her palm as the ringing tone sounded.

"Kitten," Alec's voice purred through the speaker only a few seconds later.

Keela smiled. "I've a question for you."

"Shoot."

"When we do eventually have kids, how many do you want?"

"Five," Alec instantly replied.

I stared at the phone.

"Why five?" Keela asked.

"Because I come from five... it's a thing me and my brothers have always liked. If we were to have kids, we'd all like five."

"Okay, thanks, babe. Talk to you later."

Keela hung up before Alec could say another word.

"Five fuckin' kids each."

"That's twenty Slater children if we all meet the quota," Branna mused. "Twenty-five when Damien eventually settles down."

I blew out a large breath. "Our poor fuckin' fannies."

We burst into a fit of laughter.

"So, I heard Alec grumbling about Kane not appreciatin' him eariler," Keela said to me with a raised eyebrow when our laughter subsided. "You know what that is all about?"

I laughed. "Yeah, I do."

"Do tell," Bronagh said as she ate a chocolate bar and leaned on the counter in Branna, Ryder, and Damien's kitchen. I came over with Kane so he could spar with Nico and lift weights with Alec. Bronagh and Keela tagged along with them so we were having a girly chat while they worked out.

"Earlier, in me apartment, Nico was askin' what would help me go into labour. Naturally, I listed the things that are supposed to help, but the lads zeroed in on one act in particular."

"Sex," Bronagh and Keela said in unison.

"On the money," I chuckled. "Well, I told the lads Kane is scared to have sex with me while I'm so heavily pregnant and Alec stepped up to take one for the team."

Keela burst into laughter.

"He didn't!"

"He did."

Bronagh fanned her face. "So what exactly did he do?"

"Alec offered to have sex with me to help me go into labour."

Keela snorted. "*I'll* have sex with you if it'll help you go into labour."

"Me too, I'll happily do it," Bronagh chirped.

"You will happily do what?"

We looked to the doorway when Nico and Kane walked into the kitchen. Bronagh grinned knowingly at her boyfriend.

"Me self and Keela are offerin' to have sex with Aideen to help her go into labour."

I heard a high-pitched scream come from the hallway.

"Accept!"

I stared wide-eyed as Alec skidded into the kitchen, barrelling into his brothers like they were pins and he was a bowling ball.

"Accept the proposition, Aideen," he pleaded as he tried to remain on his feet. "I've dreamt of shit like this for years!"

"I'm going to fucking kick your ass when I get up!" Nico growled from the floor.

Alec turned and kicked him in the stomach. "Shut up and let them think about this! This is important."

I laughed at Alec and looked to the girls who were shaking their heads. I decided to play with him and his brothers simply because I could use the entertainment.

"Fine, go get the dildos."

"Oh, my God." Alec placed his hands on either side of his face. "This is the best day of my life."

Keela bit down on her lower lip. "What do you want me to do to them?"

His eyes welled up. "It's finally happening."

Bronagh covered her mouth with her hand when she couldn't control the giggle that erupted from her. Alec's attention zoned in on her and her mouth.

"You ... you're playing ... aren't you?" he whispered, legit tears falling from his eyes.

Keela laughed then, too.

"That was cruel, Aideen," Alec whispered and wiped his tear stained cheeks. "So fucking cruel. Don't *ever* talk to me again. I don't like any of you anymore."

He stormed out of the kitchen with Keela laughing as she ran after him. I looked to Kane and Nico when they grunted and found them staring at me.

"What?" I asked.

Nico blinked he eyes. "You shouldn't lie like that, not about threesomes. It's hurtful."

"It's only hurtful because this is one threesome that isn't comin' true and it's killin' all of you."

Kane chimed in. "That doesn't make it any less evil to lie about it. You got poor Alec's hopes up."

"Just Alec's?" I grinned.

Kane glared at me. "Mine and Dominic's too."

"Damn right," Nico snarled.

I laughed. "You're all too easy to play with."

"You made Alec cry."

And I actually felt guilty about it.

"Alec cried yesterday when he found out KFC were updatin' their menu," Bronagh cut in. "Him cryin' isn't that big of a deal, trust me."

That knowledge instantly made me feel better.

"He is too perfect, I love him." I smiled gleefully.

Bronagh nodded in agreement. "Me too."

"Hey," Kane growled.

I rolled my eyes. "I love you, too, obviously."

Kane was appeased with that.

"Bronagh," Nico grunted.

She looked at him and said, "What?"

His lips thinned to a line. "Say you love me, too."

She smiled wide. "I love you too, Dominic."

Nico smiled then and it caused me to shake my head. For big men, with looks and personalities to die for, they needed constant reassurance from us girls that we loved them.

Either that or they just liked hearing us say it so often.

I yawned as I walked out of my bathroom. I was about to turn and head into my bedroom so I could go back to bed, when I heard a familiar voice in the kitchen. I frowned as I turned and walked down the hallway and into the room.

"Hey, Ryder," I said when I saw him sitting across from Kane at our kitchen table.

Kane raised his brows. "I thought you were already in bed."

"I was, but woke up to go to the toilet and I heard his voice and thought somethin' might be wrong. It's past midnight."

Ryder scratched his neck. "Sorry about dropping by so late."

"Is everythin' okay?" I asked, concerned.

He nodded. "Yeah, just need to talk to Kane."

I knew that was my cue to bid them a goodnight, but I looked to Kane and saw he was fully dressed when only a few hours ago he was topless and in a pair of shorts.

"Why are you dressed?" I asked, frowning.

Kane looked down at himself then to me and said, "I was just going to head out with Ryder for a bit."

"And leave me on my own?" I asked, my eyes wide with panic.

He wouldn't do that, not with Big Phil still out there.

"No," Kane instantly replied. "I was going to wake you up and drop you off at Alec's so you could sleep there with him and Keela."

I blinked. "What is so important that you would trouble them with me so late?"

Silence.

I frowned. "Kane, where are you goin'?"

Kane hesitated and glanced at Ryder who adverted his gaze.

They were up to something.

"You're stayin' here with me," I stated to Kane.

Ryder sighed and glanced to Kane. "Stay with her, I've got this."

"Are you sure?" Kane questioned.

Ryder nodded and stood up, winking at me before he left the apartment. I looked to Kane and folded my arms across my chest.

"What the hell was that?"

Kane scratched his neck. "What the hell was what?"

"Don't treat me like I'm stupid. Where were you goin' with Ryder?"

He looked away. "I don't need to tell you everything, Aideen."

"Hold on a bloody second," I snapped and grabbed hold of his jacket to stop him from walking away from me. "You *do* have to tell me because I know he is involved in drugs and God knows what else."

"What Ryder does is his business—"

"I'm with you!" I cut him off. "What you do *is* me business if it's associated with that bullshit."

Kane set his jaw. "Can't you just trust me?"

"On this?" I questioned. "No, I can't. I don't want you goin' off with Ryder."

Kane humourlessly laughed. "He's my brother."

"I don't care if he is Jesus Christ himself," I bellowed. "He is up to no good and I don't want you involved in whatever he has his hands in."

"What would you have me do?" Kane demanded. "Turn my back on my brother? The answer is hell fucking no. Being loyal is a part of who I am; I will never turn my back on my own. You *know* that."

I shook my head in disbelief. "I'm not askin' you to turn your back on Ryder, just the shit he is involved in."

"Why're you so sure he is up to something?"

That was a loaded question.

"Because you're all actin' differently. A few months ago, before I moved here, I was in your old kitchen at six in the mornin', and he and Nico were goin' somewhere so he could do some 'business'. He doesn't have a job so I *know* he is gettin' his money from somewhere," I angrily stated. "He wouldn't let up on what that was, but deep down I *knew* it was somethin' messed up. I had too much on me mind to take proper notice at the time. *Oh*, and not to mention the time that I almost sniffed cocaine that got onto my hand from his jacket in the same kitchen. Explain *that*."

Kane pinched the bridge of his nose. "I'm not telling you Ryder's business, so drop it."

I blinked at the dismissal.

"I warned you that I would not be with you if you weren't honest with me about stuff like this. I wasn't jokin' when I said I'd be gone if you went back to that life."

Kane's eyes narrowed to slits. "Don't threaten me, Aideen. You're mine."

"And I'll be yours forever, but that doesn't mean I'll stand by you while you do God knows what with your shady brother. I love Ryder, but he is an arsehole!"

Kane's eye twitched so I turned and walked away from him knowing good and well he was past the point of reason. I walked into our bedroom and over my shoulder I said, "Enjoy the sofa."

I reached for the door and turned to close it, but jumped back when Kane stepped into the room, blocking the way.

"You're not kicking me out of our bed."

"I don't want to be near you right now so yes, I am."

He didn't move.

"Don't make me choose. I can't choose between you and Ryder, I love you both."

I placed my hand over my face in despair for a moment before dropping it back to my side. "I'm not fuckin' askin' you to choose. I just don't want you helpin' Ryder with whatever it is that he has goin' on. That's it."

"He needs my help though."

I was furious.

"Just *tell* me what you're doin' with him."

Kane hesitated then sighed and said, "I can't. It's up to him whether he tells people or not."

I held up my hand.

"Last chance. Tell me where you were going to go with Ryder."

Kane was torn between his loyalty for me, and his loyalty for his brother.

"I can't, baby. Please just trust me that it's not shady. I'm just trying to help him."

I shook with anger. "I know he is involved with things from his past, and now you're too. You promised me all that was behind us."

"It is—"

"It's not!" I shouted. "*He* is still out there, and instead of tryin' to find him, you're off playin' gangster with Ryder."

"*What?*" he asked, his eyes wide with shock. "I'm putting everything I have into finding that son of a bitch. I just don't mention it to you because I don't want you so aware of the prick."

Oh.

He looked away from me. "You don't understand shit with Ryder."

"Then *help* me to."

"I. Can't. Ryder made me promise not to tell you because you would tell Branna."

It was definitely something shady.

"I *knew* it was somethin' fucked up," I spat.

"Aideen—"

"Tell me."

He stared at me, but remained mute.

"Leave!" I screamed. "Take what's yours and get the fuck out. I can't deal with this right now."

"Fine," he bellowed back and rushed me. "I'll take what's mine and go."

For a second I had no idea what was happening, but then realisation hit me. This motherfucker was trying to lift my pregnant arse up.

"Kane!" I screeched when he hooked his arm behind my knees and slide his arms around my waist and lifted me. My arms instinctively went up into the air then tightly wrapped around Kane's neck.

"What the hell do you think you're doin'?" I asked on a gasp.

He walked towards the door of our apartment. "You said to take what's mine and get the fuck out. I'm doing exactly that."

Me.

He meant me.

I was his.

For a moment I stared at him, then my heart kicked into overdrive and pleasure filled me. I'd be damned if I didn't love him and his alpha ways. I looked at him and then I started to cry.

He stopped walking.

"Why are you crying?"

"Because I love you," I stated and swatted at him. "I don't want you to leave, but I also don't want secrets between us."

Kane sighed. "I love you, too, so please just trust me when I say it's nothing I can't handle, and it will be done soon."

I swallowed. "You promise it won't take you away from me?"

"Aideen, baby, I promise," he said and kissed the side of my head. "I'm not going anywhere."

I nodded. "I'm sorry for fightin'."

I was. I wasn't happy that I still didn't know what Ryder was up to, but I respected and loved Kane too much not to take his word that he would be okay.

"Are you sorry because you're genuinely sorry, or just because you don't want me to carry you out of the apartment because it's cold outside?"

I lightly smiled. "Both."

Kane chortled and leaned his head down so he could kiss my cheek. I sighed as I played with the ends of his hair. "You wouldn't think so, but I'm so hot for you right now."

Kane looked down at me and said, "Really?"

"Oh, yes." I nodded. "I *love* when you claim me as yours. It's so sexy."

He growled and my clit suddenly pulsed to life.

"I love when you make sounds like that, too."

Kane smirked and carefully set me down on the floor. I slid my hands down his arms and licked my lips as they glided off his flexed biceps.

"I love how big you are. You make me feel tiny, which is saying something because I'm huge right now."

Kane continued to smirk. "What else is big about me that you love?"

I grinned. "I'll give you two guesses, but you're only goin' to need one."

"You can sweet talk me all you like; I'm not having sex with you."

I whimpered. "But Kane—"

"Nope. We've talked—or shouted—about this already. He is so low, I'm afraid I'll knock against his head or something."

I groaned. "Your dick isn't long enough to touch him."

"Thanks very much."

"No," I laughed. "I mean—"

"I know what you mean, but I just can't do it. He is our baby and he is so close to coming into this world. It freaks me out knowing he could move while I'm inside you. Like... he could possibly be awake while I'm banging his mom. That's not cool at all, Aideen."

I crossed my legs when laughter erupted out of me, but it was too late.

"I just peed myself!" I laughed. "This is your fault."

Kane laughed loudly as he held onto me. "Come on, pissy panties. Let's get you to the bathroom."

He took me by the hand, and as much as it killed me not knowing what he was up to, I put my trust in him like he asked because I loved him more than life itself.

The sex thing though?

That bullshit wasn't flying at all.

I would seduce Kane... even if it killed me.

CHAPTER FIVE

"Aideen?"

Not. Now.

"Baby, wake up."

I growled. "Why?"

I felt a hand touch my behind.

"It's nearly eleven. If you sleep any longer then you won't sleep tonight."

I whimpered and buried my face into my pillow. "But I'm so tired."

I was exhausted from the baby's movements keeping me awake during the night. Usually I could doze during her tossing and turning, but last night she was so tightly tucked under my ribs that it hurt to lie down. I had to stand up so I could breathe probably.

"I'm know you are, darling, but you can nap later. I promise."

Hmmm.

A nap sounded good.

"Can I nap now?" I asked, my eyes cracking open to take a peek at my surroundings.

Kane's low rumbling chuckle caused a slow smile to spread across my face.

"You aren't a morning person, are you?" he mused.

"No, I'm not. There is a reason mornin' and mournin' sound the same."

He laughed louder, then not-so-gently swatted my behind.

"Get your fine ass up."

I stayed put.

"Or what?"

Kane levelled me with a don't-fuck-with-me stare. "You don't want to know 'or what?'"

I knew he would do something I didn't like if I tested him, so I dramatically sighed as I pushed myself up to my knees and sat back on my heels. I looked to Kane and pouted.

He only smiled at me as he leaned over the bed, snaked his hand around my neck where he gripped me tightly and pulled me forward until his mouth covered mine.

I moaned into his mouth and lifted my hands to his biceps, squeezing him lightly.

"Good morning," he murmured against my lips.

I sucked on his lower lip before releasing it with a pop and saying, "Fuck me and it will be a *really* good mornin'."

Kane growled. "Aideen."

Shit.

"Please," I begged. "You know how sensitive I am. I need some simulation and release or I start to hurt."

Kane frowned. "You know I can make you come without fucking you, babydoll."

I grunted. "It's great, but not the same. I miss feelin' you inside of me."

"You're trying to guilt me," Kane said and set his jaw.

I continued to pout. "Is it workin'?"

"No," he said through clenched teeth.

I looked to the side then down and grinned when I saw his erection strained against his jeans. I reached for it, but Kane quickly grabbed hold of my wrist, halting my movements.

"Kane," I snapped, anger rising within me. "Please, just fuck me. It's been over five weeks since you pulled this no sex crap. It's not funny anymore. We should use this time to have as much sex as possible since we won't be able to for *weeks* after I have the baby!"

The muscle worked in his jaw as he glared at me, which only annoyed me further.

"I don't feel comfortable having sex with you while you're so close to having the baby."

Sadness squished my anger.

"You... you find me body uncomfortable?" I asked then looked away when tears welled in my eyes. "Do you think I'm ugly?"

Kane lowly cursed before lowering my hand that he still held to the front of his jeans, rubbing my palm over his hardened length. "Does that feel like I think your body is uncomfortable or ugly?"

I sniffled. "No."

"Look at me."

I did.

"You're the most beautiful woman I've ever laid eyes on, and you're so sexy my dick can hardly stand it. When you're swollen with my baby, it heightens my attraction to you. Your. Body. Is. Perfect."

I looked up at him. "Then why won't you take me?"

He blushed a little. "I just don't like the idea of my cock being so close to our baby. I know you have told me it's impossible to touch him, but it just... freaks me out. I'm sorry."

I was still upset, but I was also reassured that he didn't find me unattractive because I was pregnant and, well, whale sized.

"It's okay," I said even though I still wished we could have sex.

I didn't just want the orgasm that sex brought; I adored the intimacy and closeness of being so close to Kane. That's what I was starting to miss.

"Are you mad?"

Mad? No.

Upset? Yes.

"No, I'm not mad," I replied and hugged his body to mine.

I felt him relax and sigh with relief. After a minute I went into the bathroom. When I was finished going to the toilet and having a morning wash, I glanced in the mirror.

I always wanted to have sex while looking at Kane as he fucked me from behind. I placed my hands on the bathroom counter, bent forward and crossed my legs when the pulse between them intensified.

Damn it.

"What are you doing?"

I glanced to the side when I heard his voice then glanced down to my body. Clearly I wasn't being obvious enough.

"I feel really hot right now. Me clit is hurtin', and I was wonderin' if you would do somethin' for me?"

He came up behind me and eyed me suspiciously in the mirror and asked, "What do you want?"

"I want to come in this position... but with your cock stimulatin' my clit."

Kane's sharp intake of breath almost made me grin.

Almost.

"What kind of monster are you?" he accused.

I smiled innocently. "What do you mean?"

"Do you have any idea how difficult it will be for me to do what you want *without* fucking you?"

I had an idea.

"I can give you head after I come if you want?" I reasoned

Kane opened his mouth then closed it. He stared at me for a few moments before he said, "Okay," and began unbuckling the belt around his hips and unbuttoning his jeans.

I blinked.

That was easier than I thought it would be.

"I'm so excited," I squealed, making Kane snort.

I stood upright from the counter and turned when he stepped closer to me. Without speaking, he dipped his head and captured my mouth with a hungry kiss. I wound my hands around his neck and knotted my fingers in his hair causing him to growl into my mouth.

"Turn around," he ordered, his voice low and husky.

My pulsed spiked as I did what I was told.

I dropped my hands from his hair, turned around and gripped onto the counter before me. Kane kneeled down and placed his hands on the hem of my pyjamas shorts and underwear.

After one swift pull he had them around my ankles. I stepped out of them and kicked them to the side. I looked up expecting to see Kane, but I saw only me.

"Kane?"

"Bend forward a little more."

I leaned forward as much as I could without it being too uncomfortable on my stomach and back. I had to widen my stance, and gripped the countertop harder than before.

"Okay, now wha—*KANE!*"

I screamed as his warm, wet tongue suddenly plunged into my body, and his large calloused hands latched onto my thighs as he feasted on me.

I held my breath for a moment, but moaned with pleasure as Kane removed his tongue from my body, and tongued his way up to my clit. He sucked the bundle of nerves into his mouth and rubbed it back and forth between his lips causing me to throw my head back as heat flooded my core.

I was about to come.

"Kane," I cried out. "Use your cock, *please*."

He growled as he tore his mouth from my clit and stood up behind me. I heard the rustle of his jeans as he did as I pleaded. He suddenly placed his hand on my lower back and kicked my ankles with his foot, forcing me to widen my stance as much as I possibly could without it hurting.

I felt my eyes roll back when Kane slid the head of his cock against me, using my juices as lubrication.

"Fuck," he hissed through what sounded like clenched teeth. "You're so wet, baby."

I moaned in response and nudged my behind back against him.

He sucked in a breath and used both of his hands to grip my hips where he dug his fingers into my flesh in warning to be still.

"Kane, please," I begged, feeling the edge of my impending orgasm simmering down.

He lifted his right hand from my body, gripped his cock and rubbed the head back and forth over my clit.

Yes.

"Are you close?" he asked, his voice strained.

I didn't answer him.

Instead I looked up and through the mirror I caught his gaze just as I pulled forward a little. The moment I felt Kane's cock slide back to my entrance, I pushed back. Kane roared and grabbed hold of my hips, halting him breaching me completely. He looked down and almost snarled when I wiggled my behind against him, trying to take more than just his head.

"You. Are. Evil."

"No," I panted. "I'm horny and want you to fuck me."

"Aideen—"

"Watch me while you fuck me."

"*Aideen*," Kane growled in warning. "I can't."

I pouted. "Please, just try to put the head in a little more... I really need to feel you, Kane. I'm begging you."

Kane set his jaw, but his eyes fluttered shut when I rubbed back against him.

"Just... just the tip?" he whispered and cracked an eye open.

Hell. No.

I nodded my head to appease him.

"Just the tip, baby," I repeated.

I was spewing bullshit because as soon as I got the chance I would push back and take all of him.

"Oh, fuck," Kane snarled. "This is... God!"

I quivered as goose bumps broke out over my skin. "Yes, just a little more."

Kane's fingers dug into my hips. "You aren't making this... easier. Fuck. *How* do you feel tighter?"

I licked my lips. "Lack of use, maybe?"

Kane slapped my arse and said, "Smartass."

I grinned to myself, taking him that bit deeper instead as he gently pushed his hips forward. He hissed as if he were in pain. He *would* be in pain if he didn't give in to his body's needs and take me.

Taking things into my own hands, or vagina, with all of my might I pushed back and in one fluid motion Kane was balls deep inside of me. He roared as his hands squeezed me tightly. He held still for all of two-seconds before he lost it.

"Fuck! I'm sorry, son."

His control was a thing of the past; he pounded into me so hard I thought I would split in two.

"Is this what you wanted?" he snarled as he leaned forward and bit down on my shoulder.

I arched my back and moaned out loud, "Yes."

Kane's hands were all over me as he fucked me. I couldn't let go of the counter with my hands to reach back and feel for him because without the balance, I would fall flat on my face.

"God, I've missed this pussy," he grunted as he slammed into me.

I gripped the counter tighter as I felt my orgasm stir back up inside of me.

"Yes, yes!" I cried out. "Kane, fuck!"

"Look at me."

I lifted my gaze to the mirror and watched his face twist with pleasure as he bore his eyes into mine.

"Are you with me?" he asked, his eyes so hooded with ecstasy they almost closed.

I pushed back into him and closed my eyes. "Always."

He picked up his pace and fucked me so hard I momentarily stopped breathing as my body exploded. I greedily sucked in air when my lungs began to burn. My grip on the counter loosened as the toe-curling pulses slowed and my hips stopped jerking.

"Wow," I whispered, and pressed my cheek to the cool marble countertop.

I shivered as I felt Kane slide out of me, his hands still on my hips.

"Fuck," he groaned. "That was awesome."

I hummed in agreement.

I was still recovering when I heard Kane move about then suddenly jumped when a wet, cool piece of fabric pressed between my legs.

"Easy," Kane murmured. "I'm just cleaning you up, I came more than usual."

I tiredly chuckled. "That's what happens when you deny yourself sex, your balls explode when you give in."

Kane guffawed as he continued to gently wipe me clean before placing the cloth he used in the wash basket in the corner of the bathroom. I stood upright as he came up behind me and put his arms around me. He nuzzled the side of his face against mine, and slid his hands over my belly.

"I can't believe you seduced me."

I giggled. "I can't believe it took so long for me to successfully seduce you. Usually I just have to look at you the right way and you're game."

He nipped my shoulder. "I was worried about the little one."

I covered my hands with his. "Sex is recommended towards the end of pregnancy. I told you. A lot of the time it can be the very thing to induce labour."

Kane looked up at me through the mirror and said, "What are we waiting for then? Bedroom. Now."

I laughed as he grabbed my hand and pulled me out of the bathroom. With a determined look on his face, and one of pure delight on mine, we headed to our sanctum.

The prospect of going into labour early never looked, or felt, so good.

"Where are James, Harley and Dante?" I asked Gavin as I held my phone to my ear.

I was so relieved that he answered his phone and that he was at home instead of out with his stupid friend Jason Bane getting up to God only knows what. I was sat on my bed talking to my Gavin because all of Kane's brothers were in our sitting room and I got the sudden urge to hear from one of my lads. They were always over visiting, but not as much as the Slater brothers and it just made me miss them.

I was bored too.

I would usually spend the evening time correcting my students' homework, but since I was on maternity leave I had nothing to do in regards to work, and I missed it.

I missed my students.

I was entitled to twenty-six weeks of paid maternity leave with an additional sixteen weeks of unpaid maternity leave if I needed more time at home.

Typically, women would take two weeks off before the impending birth of their child, but as it was so flexible in my job, I tapped into eight of the sixteen unpaid weeks I had and used them after I was attacked, which the school was more than happy to accommodate.

I sighed as I pushed away thoughts of how much I missed working, and focused on the phone call to my brother.

"James and Harley are on a *blind* double date, and Dante is here with me playing Fifa."

That fucking game. Kane and his brothers were playing the same game constantly.

"Tell Dante hey."

"Tell him yourself, puttin' you on speaker now."

I smiled. "Dante, why are you playin' video games with Gavin on a Friday night instead of being out?"

Dante's snort was loud. "Hello to you too, dear sister."

I grinned.

"To answer your question, it's only half ten, I don't go anywhere until twelve. No one goes to clubs when they just open."

I rolled my eyes. "I can't remember the last time I went clubbin' so spare me the details."

My brothers laughed.

"Are you still pregnant?" Gavin asked me.

I smiled. "No, I had the kid and decided not to tell you both."

Dante snickered. "You walked right into that one."

"Whatever. When do you think you will have the baby? You've been pregnant forever."

Tell me about it.

"I've two weeks until me due date, it might be a while yet."

They both sighed and it made me smile.

"I miss you both."

Dante snorted. "You saw me two days ago."

"Two days is a *long* time," I countered.

"I'll swing by tomorrow, that cool?"

I nodded even though he couldn't see me.

I opened my mouth to speak when I heard Gavin growl, "Fuckin' Nico."

"What?" I questioned as cheers erupted from my sitting room.

"The prick just scored against me."

I blinked. "Are you playing Kane and his brothers?"

"Yeah, we're takin' turns," Dante replied.

Boys and their bloody toys.

"Okay, I'll leave you both be." I frowned. "See you tomorrow."

"Bye," Gavin's voice sounded before the phone clicked off.

Goodbye to you, too, little brother.

I shook my head, tossed my phone onto my nightstand and stood up. I was bored, and even though I didn't want to watch the lads play their football game, it beat lying in bed doing nothing.

The girls, bar Branna who was working, went out for dinner and because it was a restaurant that served sushi, I couldn't go. Sushi was off limits to me. It made me sick before I was pregnant. Even the smell of it could set me off, but it was a definite no-go now that I was having a baby.

I exited my room and paused at the front door as a key entered the lock and the handle jiggled. I stepped back with a racing heart until I saw who the person was and calmed down.

"Keela," I breathed. "You scared me."

She looked just as surprised to see me standing right behind the door, but quickly exhaled and moved closer to me.

"How was dinner—"

"I need your help."

I widened my eyes. "With what?"

"The girls," Keela murmured.

I gasped. "What about the girls?"

"Shhh!"

I winced and looked to the sitting room door as it opened and Nico and Kane practically fell out of it. Kane placed his hand on his chest when he saw me.

"Fuck. I thought something was wrong."

I looked to Keela who was glaring at me.

"My bad."

Nico straightened. "Keela, where are Bronagh and Alannah?"

She scratched her neck. "In the elevator."

I poked her arm.

"What's wrong?"

She groaned. "It's not me fault, I didn't know what they were drinkin'—"

"Keela?" Alec's voice said sternly from behind his brothers. "What happened?"

I blinked at Alec, having never heard him sound so serious before.

"Brongah and Alannah, they're kind of... drunk."

Nico stumbled. "Bronagh is *pregnant*!"

"Yeah," Keela said and scratched her neck again. "We were at dinner and her and Alannah drank these weird drinks. The menu said they were alcohol free ... but they weren't. The waiter got the order mixed up. She didn't drink loads, just a few glasses."

Nico raised an eyebrow. "Where the hell is she? I can deal with her—"

"Promise you won't get mad?"

"Keela," Nico said, his tone dangerously low. "Where is Bronagh?"

Keela caved under his gaze. "I told you she is in the elevator ... but she is sittin' in it in just her bra and knickers, ridin' it up and down with Alannah... who is also drunk, and semi-naked."

Damien was suddenly pushing his way through his brothers so fast it made Kane laugh.

"Semi-naked, drunk Alannah?" he said. "Damien Slater is on the case."

All the brothers laughed, but the twins ignored them and ran out of the apartment. I followed them just because I wanted to see the next few minutes unfold. I walked up behind Damien and Nico and folded my arms across my chest when Nico hit the elevator button.

"It's on the second floor and rising," Damien murmured.

We all watched the dial for the floors, and watched the number climb higher and higher until the elevator pinged and the double doors opened. I covered my hands with my mouth when I saw what I saw.

"Nope," Bronagh slurred. "Your ti-tits are *definitely* bigger than mine."

"Really?" Alannah murmured and cupped her boobs in her hands. "I don't think th-they are."

What in the world?

"Oh, my God." I laughed.

Nico cursed when he took her in. "Damn it, Bronagh!"

Bronagh and Alannah turned their heads and burst into giggles when they saw the three of us staring at them.

"We're caught," Alannah shouted and put her hands in the air. "Elevator lesbian sex is no more!"

Damien balled his hand into a fist, brought it to his mouth and bit down on it. I didn't know whether he wanted to laugh at her or if he was stopping himself from taking her right then and there.

His gaze was solely locked on her.

"Damien!" Alannah squealed with excitement when her eyes landed on him and she pushed herself to her feet.

I watched her with wide eyes because she only had a black pair of underwear on.

That was it.

"Yes, Alannah?" he asked and made a point of keeping eye contact with her.

She cupped her bare breasts with both hands. "Do my boobs look bigger than the la-last time you saw them?"

Nico stepped in the way of the elevator doors when they tried to close. He hit the emergency stop button and stared down at his girlfriend.

"I can't believe this shit," he grunted and put his right hand up like a fan on the side of his face to form a divide so he couldn't see Alannah's body.

"Damien," Alannah pressed, "do they or don't th-they?"

I looked at Damien and the poor bastard was staring at Alannah's chest like it was his next meal. I elbowed him and he looked at me before clearing his throat and looking to Alannah's face.

"Um, why don't we get you dressed? Does that sound good?"

Alannah lazily smirked. "Will *you* be the one to dress me?"

"You. Me. Crazy elevator sex. Right no-now."

I looked to Bronagh when she spoke and laughed when she grabbed hold of Dominic's shoulders and pulled him down on top of her body.

"Bronagh!" he shouted with surprise. "I could hurt you. Would you let me get you dressed and we—"

"You told me you loved me naked th-though."

Nico grunted. "I do, but—"

"Then let me be naked, I like being free," she said, and shimmied causing her breasts, and other places, to jiggle.

I cackled and took out my phone, and began recording. There was no way in hell I was *not* capturing this.

"Bronagh, for the love of God, *stop* doing that," Nico begged as he adjusted the front of his trousers.

"Shimmy with me!" she giggled, making me laugh harder.

Nico pressed his face onto the crown of her head as his shoulders shook and he laughed. I switched the phone to Damien and saw he, too, was laughing as Alannah tried to twerk.

I say tried because she failed, she *miserably* failed. I crisscrossed my legs and howled with laughter. It got the interest of the occupants inside my apartment.

"What are they doin'?" Keela's voice called out from behind me.

I glanced over my shoulder, and with my free hand I waved because I couldn't speak. I could barely breathe from laughing.

"Alannah!" Keela gasped when she came to my side and saw what she was doing.

Damien lifted her shirt from the floor and held it in front of her when his brothers came up behind us. He narrowed his eyes at them and Ryder laughed.

"You being protective, little brother?"

Damien kept his eyes narrowed. "They aren't decent. You, Alec and Kane go back inside the apartment."

"No!" Alannah shouted in protest. "Let's have an or-orgy. Right here in the elevator. All of us."

I shoved my phone at Keela to continue recording for me so I could bend forward and ease the sudden pain in my side. Hands gripped onto my hips.

"Aideen?" Kane murmured, his voice filled with concern.

I shook my head. "I just have... a stitch," I said, laughing. "They're so funny."

"I don't think I've seen so much of Alannah's skin before," Alec murmured, "and I've definitely never heard her talk about sex before. She must be really drunk to want an orgy with all of us."

Kane laughed at his brother, but nodded in agreement.

I looked to Nico when he got Bronagh to her feet and managed to get her t-shirt back over her head. He was in the middle of putting her arms through the holes and tugging it down to her hips.

"Nearly done, pretty girl."

Bronagh turned her nose up. "Don't call me Bronagh or pretty girl anymore."

Nico smiled down at her. "What will I call you if not Bronagh or my pretty girl?"

She looked him dead in the eyes and said, "From th-this moment onwards I shall be known as MC Hammered."

I burst into a fit of laughter and stumbled back into Kane's vibrating chest. He folded his arms around me and rested his hands on top of my bump, and his chin on top of my head.

"Okay, MC Hammered, you wanna put your hands on my shoulders so I can put your pants back on you?"

Bronagh stared at Nico for a long moment then said, "I want to get ma-married."

Oh, shit.

All traces of laughter evaporated and heavy silence lingered.

"You want to get married?" Nico repeated as if he misheard her.

Bronagh nodded her head. "We're to-together forever, we live together ag-ages and we're havin' a baby. I love you with all of my heart. The wh-whole lot of it. I want to get married, so will you marry me?"

Nico was still then said, "Yeah, babe, I'll marry you."

I beamed and clapped my hands together with excitement.

"Yes!" Bronagh said and high-fived herself. "I lo-love you."

I giggled. "She won't remember this tomorrow."

Kane kissed the crown of my head. "No, but we will."

"I love you too, MC Hammered," Nico said making us laugh, and Bronagh beam.

We watched them embrace for a moment until Alannah cleared her throat.

"Does no one wa-want to have sex with me?" she asked, sounding tired. "I promise I'm good at it."

All eyes fell on Damien.

He glared at us. "Thanks very much, guys!"

I grinned. "We got you."

He hissed at me then looked to Alannah who had sunk down to the floor of the elevator. Damien knelt before her and picked up her discarded leggings and put her feet through the leg holes. He lifted her hands and placed them over her breasts then slowly pulled the leggings up to her knees then gripped her elbows. He pulled her to her feet, as he remained on his knees before her.

Alannah tilted her head to the side and frowned down at him. "You took th-them off me before and now you're puttin' them back on ... ha-have we come full circle?"

Damien stilled then pressed his forehead against her bare thighs before gripping the hem of her leggings and shimmying them up until they fit snug around her hips. He picked up her bra and t-shirt and blocked her from our view with his body.

I saw Alannah drop her arms from covering her chest and Damien looked up to the ceiling before returning his gaze to her. He put her bra on, then got her shirt on her and buttoned it up.

When he was done, he was going to step away from her—I saw him prepare to take the step backward, but Alannah suddenly stepped forward and fell against his chest. Damien caught her and looked down to her face, before sighing.

"How the hell can she go from asking people for sex, to falling asleep on me standing up?"

Keela pocketed my phone and said, "They drank some weird shit. Fruity cocktails. There wasn't much alcohol in them when I asked the staff because I was wonderin' what had them so giddy. There was hardly any alcohol at all, I was assured... they're just lightweights."

Bronagh suddenly laughed. "I'm not a lightweight, as-ask Dominic. I can dr-drink *loads*."

Nico was walking out of the elevator and when Bronagh spoke he looked at us and shook his head before smiling at Bronagh. "Of course you can, babe."

I snorted.

He was so whipped.

We followed the lads back into my apartment then Kane pulled out the sofa bed. We laughed when both girls instantly starting snoring after the twins set them down on it.

"Leave them here tonight," I said to the twins. "I'll look after them."

Nico hesitated, but nodded his head.

Damien scratched his neck. "Should we call someone about Alannah though?"

I shook my head. "She lives on her own, you don't need to call anyone."

"No boyfriend?"

Ryder grinned. "She's single."

Damien didn't reply, but the look of relief on his face was evident.

It caused me to smile as he grabbed the large blanket from the back of the sofa and laid it out over the girls. We all stared at them for a minute until Alec and Keela turned, said their goodbyes and filed out of the apartment. Ryder checked his phone and followed suit.

Nico and Damien hovered for a few more minutes, but when I assured them I'd take good care of the girls, they gave in, hugged me and left.

"You can go on to bed, babe," Kane said. "I'm gonna play Fifa some more."

I nodded my head and looked to the girls, smiling at their snores. Their skin glowed as the twinkling lights of the Christmas tree and various decorations around the room shone upon their sleeping forms.

"I'll sleep out here, too," he said and nodded to the one sitter he always sat on. "Just to keep my eyes on them while you get some sleep."

I smiled. "You're the best."

He devilishly grinned. "We'll swap in the morning when they wake up."

At that thought the smile left my face and worry took over because realisation hit that I would have to deal with hung-over Bronagh *and* Alannah all on my lonesome.

Fuck me.

CHAPTER SIX

"Holy Mary Mother of God, I'm dyin'!"

I smiled as I stirred two sugars into the two Christmas printed cups of tea before me. I put the spoon into the sink when I was finished and glanced at a packet of painkillers Kane left out on the counter before he went to bed this morning when Bronagh and Alannah woke up groaning in pain.

I gripped the handles of the cups and left my kitchen and entered the sitting room, shaking my head at Bronagh and Alannah who were both still on the sofa bed, but both were buried under the blanket that covered them.

"I have tea," I announced, keeping my voice low.

Both of the girls grunted.

I placed the cups on the coffee table without uttering another word. I went back into the kitchen and checked on the fry-up I had cooking. The eggs were scrambled, the sausages, rashers, pudding and hash browns were cooked and ready to serve.

I turned off my cooker, dished up two plates for the girls and put a cover over the remaining food for Kane when he woke up. I brought the plates into the sitting room and stood at the door for a few seconds. I grinned to myself when I heard both of the girls sniffing.

"Are you able to eat?" I questioned.

Bronagh popped her head out from under the blanket. "I've puked four times since I woke up, I should be able to stomach somethin' now."

I walked over to her and waited for her to sit upright and adjust cushions behind her before I handed her the plate of food that would cure her hangover.

"Alannah?"

She groaned but came out from hiding under the blanket and sat up like Bronagh. I walked around to her and handed her the food, smiling when she licked her lips.

I adjusted a few of the ornaments on my Christmas tree then refocused on Alannah and frowned at her.

"You okay?"

She lightly shook her head and winced as if the action hurt.

"No, me head is bangin'."

I went back into the kitchen and grabbed the packet of painkillers from the counter and returned next to Alannah, holding the packet out to her.

Her shoulders sagged with relief as she offered me a pained smile and accepted the packet.

I chuckled. "You'll be fine in a few hours."

She popped two tablets from the packet, placed them in her mouth then reached for her tea and took a few test sips before gulping some down.

"Hmmmm," she moaned. "You make a mean cuppa, Ado. It's really good."

My chest swelled with pride. That was practically the best compliment an Irish person could ever receive.

"Thanks." I smiled, feeling a little smug.

Bronagh copied Alannah's actions and swallowed down some painkillers with her tea and moaned with delight when the liquid slid down her throat.

"She's right, these are even better than Ryder's and Branna has taught him well."

I was pretty proud of myself as I sat in Kane's one seater and watched the girls eat their food.

"I'm so embarrassed about last night," Alannah mumbled before chowing down some of her hash brown.

I smiled. "You were drunk."

"We were legless," Bronagh corrected. "I can't even remember some of the shit we did. I don't care what that waiter said either, they weren't *just* fruity cocktails."

Alannah mutely nodded in agreement then flicked her eyes to me. "I remember certain parts, but not everythin'... how bad was I?"

I rubbed my jaw. "The truth?"

She nodded.

"You asked us all to strip naked for an orgy, then you got mad when no one did and proceeded to ask someone to have sex with you and said that you were really good at it. It went on for a bit."

"Oh, Christ," Alannah whimpered and covered her face with her hands.

I gnawed on my inner cheek. "You also were in just your knickers and everyone saw your tits. You asked Dame if they were bigger than the last time he saw them."

"Oh, fucking hell," she shouted but quickly grabbed ahold of her head.

I looked to Bronagh and found her looking at me.

"What did I do?" she asked, her expression fearful.

I snorted. "Tried to rape Nico in the elevator, asked him to shimmy with you ... oh, you titled yourself MC Hammered, too, which was pretty funny."

Bronagh flushed crimson. "I'll never live this down."

"*You* won't?" Alannah grumbled. "I can never look the Slater brothers in the eye ever again."

Bronagh was quiet as she ate some food and did some obvious thinking. I saw her eyes well up with tears just as she said, "Do you think I hurt the baby with the alcohol?"

"Honey," I sighed. "You only had a few glasses; the baby will be perfectly fine. Don't worry yourself, do you hear me?"

Bronagh nodded her head, wiped her eyes and continued to eat her food. I lowered my hand to my belly as the baby began to move around, but I quickly snapped my gaze back to Bronagh when she gasped. I watched her knife and fork fall onto her plate as she flung her hands over her mouth.

"What is it?" Alannah asked, panicked.

"I asked Dominic to marry me!" Bronagh hollered.

I erupted with laughter. "I forgot about that."

Bronagh growled. "How could you forget somethin' like *that*?"

I shrugged. "I was thinkin' of all the funny shit you both said and did."

Bronagh's eyes were wild. "I can't believe I asked him that. I can't fuckin' believe it."

I raised a brow. "Do you *want* to marry him?"

"What do—"

"Do you want to marry him?"

Bronagh blinked. "Yes, I love him."

"Then it's a done deal. He said yes anyway."

Bronagh gasped again. "Did he really?"

I nodded. "Yep, you asked him to marry you and he said yes."

She scrambled off the chair and practically dove for my house phone. She grabbed the phone, pressed on the buttons and placed it to her ear.

After a few seconds she said, "Did you say yes to marryin' me last night? 'Cause Aideen said you did."

No hello, just straight to the point.

I watched as Bronagh suddenly burst into tears.

"Are you playin'?" she asked Nico.

Nico's response caused her to squeal.

She spun to me. "He was serious, we're engaged."

I got up and gave her a big hug followed by Alannah doing the same thing. Bronagh hung up the phone after Nico promised to come right over for her.

Bronagh turned to me and swallowed. "You don't feel like I stole your thunder, do you?"

I blinked. "Come again?"

"You and Kane just got engaged, and now me and Dominic. I'm sorry I asked him so close to Kane askin' you—"

"Don't say another word, you eejit. I'm delighted for you both."

Bronagh relaxed and gave me another hug. We sat back down after clearing away the girl's food and putting the plates into the dishwasher.

"Do you want to see it?" I asked.

"See what?" Bronagh and Alannah replied in unison.

I took my phone out of my housecoat pocket and wiggled it in their faces.

"The video I recorded of you two last night."

The look of terror that passed over both their faces caused me to laugh, loudly.

"You... you recorded us in that state?" Bronagh asked, both annoyed and shocked.

I nodded my head. "I couldn't help it, you were both hilarious."

"I don't want to see it," Alannah grunted.

Bronagh folded her arms across her chest. "Me either."

I playfully rolled my eyes. "I'm not goin' to show it to anyone... except—"

"Except?" Alannah cut me off, her brows drawn together.

"Except I may have sent it to Gavin last night, but he deleted it after he watched it because he said you were both his friends and he wouldn't be involved in slaggin' you both."

"For God's sake," Alannah grumbled and put her face in her hands.

"Delete the video." This was from Bronagh.

I frowned. "But it's funny—"

"Aideen." Both girls cut me off.

I huffed as I tapped on the screen of my phone and brought up the option to delete the video. Before I tapped delete, I looked to both of the girls one more time and said, "You both sure?"

"Yeah."

I sighed and deleted the video, then pocketed my phone.

"You both suck."

"The mortification I'll live with is what sucks," Alannah mumbled.

I gnawed on my lower lip and said, "It wasn't that bad ..."

She cut me off with a stare so I said, "Okay, it was, but you were *drunk*."

"Like that matters to the brothers," she mumbled.

We sat down and watched some television, only chatting here and there in lowered voices as we waited for the painkillers to kick in. Twenty minutes after taking them, the brunt of their pain had eased off which was perfect timing as the hall door to my apartment opened and a voice shouted, "Where is my phat ass *fiancée* at?"

Bronagh squealed—it caused Alannah to plug her ears with her fingers—and scrambled off the bed as she ran towards the sitting room door. Nico appeared in the doorway and laughed as he caught Bronagh who jumped on him when she was close enough to do so.

Bronagh covered Nico's mouth with her own, and kissed him long and hard. It caused me to clear my throat and say, "I'm happy for you both, but get a fuckin' room."

They separated and laughed, but before Nico set Bronagh down on the ground, he gave her arse a squeeze and glanced over his shoulder.

"Are you coming in or what?"

I cringed when Damien walked into the room and leaned against the doorframe.

He ignored Nico, lifted his hand and gestured with his finger for Bronagh to come to him. Bronagh practically floated over to him.

"Congrats, *sis*," Damien murmured before wrapping her up in his arms, hugging her body to his.

Bronagh hugged him back and laughed when he gave her behind a squeeze purely for Nico's benefit.

"I swear to God," Nico mumbled to himself.

Alannah was on her feet and in the middle of pushing the sofa bed back into the chair. It went in smoother when Nico helped her. She avoided looking at him and busied herself with placing the cushions back in their original positions. When she finished that, she folded up the blanket that covered herself and Bronagh throughout the night then she laid it on the back of the sofa.

Damien remained by the doorway and followed her movements with his eyes. He looked over his shoulder when my apartment door opened. He nodded his head in a 'what's up' gesture and moved aside to let the visitor into the sitting room.

When I saw my brother Gavin, I mentally snorted.

Everyone had a damn key to my place.

"What's the story?" Gavin asked the room, grinning at Alannah and Bronagh.

Alannah flushed and looked away from him while Bronagh narrowed her eyes.

"Please don't do or say somethin' that will have everyone sendin' me back to anger management."

Gavin laughed and held up his hands. "I'm not openin' me mouth."

Bronagh looked to me and grinned. "You've taught him well."

"It's what I do."

She snorted and sat down on the sofa next to Nico and Alannah.

Gavin came over to me and sat on the arm of the chair I was sitting on. He leaned down and kissed my head in greeting. I moved closer to him and leaned against his chest.

I was meaning to ask the little shite if he had backed off from Brandon's circle, but I remembered that Keela assured me her uncle was weeding Gavin out without him knowing it. He respected my decision that I wanted what was best for my brother, and that his gang was *not* it.

"Damien," Nico sighed. "Why're you standing over there?"

Damien shrugged, still staring at Alannah who was pretending to pick dirt from under her nails.

Nico glanced to Alannah then back to Damien and said, "Come on, you two. Is this how it's goin' to be every time you are both in a room at the same time?"

Alannah clenched one of her hands in a fist and said, "Drop it, Nico."

He did, but wasn't pleased to do so.

"Hi Alannah," Damien suddenly said.

She refused to look at him as she grumbled, "I wish we were social media accounts. Preferably Twitter."

Damien furrowed his eyebrows in confusion. "Uh, why?"

"So I could un-follow you in real life and have zero interaction with you. I want it so you would never be able to think or freely speak of last night's... events."

"You could still do that," Damien grinned, "but it would be called first degree murder."

I snorted, but looked away when Alannah shot me a glare with her still bloodshot eyes.

"Sorry," I mumbled.

Gavin draped his arm over my shoulder. "I'm enjoying it," he murmured. "She was so quiet in school, I wouldn't believe what she did if you hadn't shown me that video."

Damien snapped his neck in our direction.

"Aideen!" he bellowed.

Fuck.

"They made me delete it... besides, it not like it was zoomed in on their bits."

Gavin snorted. "Still a quality video without seein' them... I didn't know you could twerk, Alannah."

She couldn't, he was slagging her.

Nico lowly chuckled, but looked away when Damien pinned him with a glare.

"I wish the ground would open up and swallow me whole." Alannah sniffled. "This is the second most embarrassin' thing ever to happen to me."

"What's the first?" Gavin asked.

I elbowed him, and he grabbed at the point of pain on his body and hissed at me through clenched teeth.

"Arsehole!"

I grinned, but Damien only worked his jaw before looking at Alannah who had her face in her hands. "Look, Aideen deleted the video. No one else will see it, and I'll warn everyone else not to bring it up again, okay?"

Alannah was silent for a moment then she looked up. "Why do you want to help me?" she asked Damien.

He blinked. "Because I want to be your friend, Alannah."

"Little late for that, don't you think?"

Damien was silent. "Look, I'm very sorry for what I did—"

"Stop, Damien," Alannah whispered. "Not here, not now."

Damien closed his mouth and gave a firm nod.

Things got awkward then.

"I'm goin' to go home and die in the peace of me own apartment," Alannah rumbled.

"I'll drive you home," Kane's voice suddenly stated.

We all looked at the doorway and saw Kane standing behind Damien, fully dressed. He winked at me in greeting, earning a smile from me.

Alannah nodded her head without looking at him. She moved over to me, hugged me and kissed my cheek. "Call me if you go into labour, otherwise let me die with this hangover in peace."

I saluted her. "Aye, boss."

She lightly smiled at me before she hugged Gavin and pinched his arm, which had him hissing and calling her an arsehole like he did me. She grinned at him before standing upright.

"Thanks for helpin' me last night," she muttered to Damien then walked out of the apartment. Kane grabbed his car keys and jogged out after her.

Damien slumped down onto the sofa after the door to the apartment clicked shut. "She hates me."

I got up and moved over to the sofa, and sat next to him.

"She doesn't hate you, Dame... she's still hurt, and just confused. This is hard for her too. You've been gone for so long."

He was silent then and I looked at Bronagh and Nico who were frowning at him. I caught Nico's attention and jerked my head giving him the signal to leave with Bronagh. He nodded once then made up an excuse that had him and Bronagh saying their goodbyes and exiting my apartment.

I looked at Damien.

"Talk to me."

He was silent for so long that I thought he wasn't going to open up, but he shocked me when he started speaking.

"I left for her."

I blinked at the sudden admission and Gavin stood up when Damien spoke.

"I'll go make tea while you both talk," he said and left the room, closing the door behind him.

I looked back to Damien and said, "Explain that."

He didn't look at me as he said, "I'm sure you've heard what a prick I used to be to girls when I was a kid?"

I wasn't going to lie so I nodded my head.

"I behaved the way I did because it was the only connection with other people that I could control. After my parents died... I was a wreck. My brothers have shielded me from all the shit as we grew up, so I didn't hate my parents like they did. I had a girlfriend... I didn't know it at the time but she was pregnant. She was killed when the shit storm with Trent started."

I listened as Damien spoke, my throat sealed with emotion. I hurt badly for him. I cried my eyes out when Kane went into detail a few months ago about the things Damien went through.

"I wanted to go back to New York to make peace with her, and in my own way, I did."

"Did you find her?" I whispered.

He nodded. "She was buried in a grave marked for Trent, Marco Miles' nephew. I had the headstone removed and replaced with the correct information. I... I had an angel poem put on it, too, for our baby. I don't know if a heartbeat even developed when Nala was killed, but it was a baby that was part of me. It was mine, you know?"

I absentmindedly placed my hand on my stomach.

"I wasn't ready to be a dad, I'm still not, but I would have stepped up if Nala wasn't killed and had the baby. I wouldn't have left New York, I would have stayed and took care of them."

Tears spilled over the brim of my eyes.

"Of course you would have, honey," I assured him. "No matter the things you have done, it doesn't change that you are a good person. You left your family just so Alannah wouldn't have to be hurt when she saw you. I know you also left to make things right for Nala, but you had Alannah's best interest at heart, too."

Damien licked his lips. "I didn't just leave for Alannah. I left for me, too. I needed to figure shit out for myself, without my brothers helping me in some way like they have always done. I needed to fix me on my own."

I pushed my hair out of my face. "And did you figure out what you needed to?"

"Yeah," he nodded. "I've made peace that I can't change the past, but I can shape my future. I can be a good person and not use my exterior to manipulate people like I've done in the past. I'm in control, no one else."

I reached over and pressed my lips to his cheek.

"You're a good man, Damien."

He looked at me and smiled. "Why did Kane have to meet you before I did?"

I giggled. "Shut up, I'm a lot older than you."

He laughed and threw his arm around my shoulder. "It's probably for the best. I don't think I could handle you anyway. You're too experienced for me."

I was shaking with laughter because we both knew the kid could run circles around me with the amount of partners he has had, while I could count all the men I've ever slept with on one hand.

After we chatted about lighter stuff, Gavin came back into the room as Damien flicked through the stations on the television, and together we watched a film. I leaned my head on Damien's shoulder and he relaxed against me. I understood him more in the last few minutes than I ever did when Kane spoke to me about him, and what I learned caused my heart great pain. Damien was a troubled man, and he was trying to right his wrongs.

I knew the only thing that was keeping him a prisoner to himself was Alannah. Until things were okay with them, I doubted he would be truly happy. I wanted to help in some way, but I knew he needed to do it on his own.

He needed to break away from the protective arms of his brothers and branch out.

The only problem was, I didn't know if they would let him.

CHAPTER SEVEN

"I'll be back in a few hours, okay?"

I nodded to Kane as I took a sip of my water. "Okay."

He kissed my head then turned and left the house, leaving me in the sitting room with Nico, Alec, and Damien while Branna was in the kitchen.

"I bet you fifty euros he hurts himself," Nico murmured to his brothers.

Damien snorted. "I know he will so I'm not taking that bet."

"What are you both talkin' about?"

Nico shrugged. "He hasn't worked out properly in a while... he has been on edge since you got hurt, so he will go hard with Ryder during their session."

I blinked. "He'll know not to overdo it."

I hoped.

I didn't want him injuring himself.

"He'll pull something, I've no doubt about it in my mind."

I grunted. "I'm about two seconds away from followin' him and makin' him stay home, and I don't want to do that because he has hardly left my side over the last few weeks so change the bloody topic."

"Your leg," Alec suddenly blurted. "How is your leg?"

I mentally laughed at him, he looked so damn proud of himself for changing the topic so quickly.

"It's fine," I said and bent and straightened it out. "It gets a bit stiff sometimes, but it doesn't hurt or anythin'."

"And your arm?" Damien asked.

I looked down to my forearm and grimaced at the nasty burn scar that marred it.

"The only thing painful about it now is lookin' at it."

"What about your throat?" This came from Nico.

I snorted at the three brothers.

"I'm talkin' so it's fine. I'm fine. Perfectly fine."

They nodded their heads but kept staring at me.

I was about to laugh and question why they were staring at me until something happened.

Something wet and sudden.

I widened my eyes. As quick as I could, I jumped to my feet. I gasped and held under my belly as water gushed from between my thighs.

"Oh, shit," Nico whispered as he stared at me with wide eyes. "*Please* tell me that's not what I think it is?"

I couldn't respond, my throat was clogged up with shock.

"Bro!" Alec hissed at Nico. "She is *pregnant*, don't make fun of her for pissing herself. The baby is pressing on her bladder, have a heart!"

Alec looked at me then and smiled. "Don't even worry about it, gorgeous, we'll help get you cleaned up and—"

"Branna," I called out, my voice shaking.

Silence.

Damien opened his mouth when he realised what just happened and called her name louder. "*Branna!*"

Alec shook his head. "Why do you three look like you've seen a ghost? It's only piss—ew, why does it smell funny?"

I looked down to the clear liquid that was puddled around my feet. I gasped when more of the liquid flowed down my legs. It was the oddest sensation of not being able to stop it.

"Branna!" I called out again.

I heard the toilet flush from down the hallway. "I'm comin', just washing me hands, honey."

I took a few deep breaths then cried out when a sudden sharp cramping pain filled my mid-section. It was so painful and out of the blue that I slipped on the water that I stood in. I almost fell over, but Damien and Alec shot up from the sofa and each quickly grabbed one of my arms. They steadied me and tried to avoid standing in the water that was still dripping from me.

I could feel it.

"Oh, shit," Alec whispered then turned his head and screamed, "Branna, it's happening. Get your midwife ass in here!"

I heard an excited squeal come from the hallway, then quick-paced footsteps. Branna entered my sitting room, looked at the brothers on either side of me then to the water on my legs and at my feet.

A wide smile spread across her face. "Your water broke before your contractions started? That is brilliant, sweetheart."

"I just had a sharp pain right after they broke," I explained. "It only lasted for a few seconds though, is that bad?"

Branna shook her head. "Nope, usually contractions happen for a few hours, then your waters break, they intensify and bam, you're a mammy."

I blinked as fear suddenly filled me. "Why didn't I get the hours of contractions first? Why did my waters go first?"

Branna chuckled and the brothers moved me out of the puddle I had created to a dry patch of floor. "Every labour is different, babe. You might a have a really quick labour, or you might be in labour until tomorrow or the next day. It all depends on how fast this little one wants to come out."

"You swear this is normal?" I asked, suddenly shaking. "I still have two weeks to go. Can I not have a home birth anymore, do I have to go to the hospital?"

"Calm down, you don't need to go anywhere unless I say so."

Branna placed her hands on my cheeks and smiled into my face. "Honey, you and the baby are fine. For about three in one hundred women their waters will break before they're thirty-seven weeks along, and you're at the thirty-eight week mark. Like I said, every pregnancy is different; there is no by-the-book way to have a baby. All of what I do is simply checkin' on you and the baby throughout your labour. I follow the guidelines your body sets. This is perfectly normal and nothing to worry about, I promise you."

I nodded my head, and took a few breaths to try and calm myself.

"I'm going to switch into midwife mode now, okay?" Branna smiled.

I nodded and found myself smiling when Nico and Alec kissed my head in unison, followed by Damien who kissed my nose.

"Let's do this, Ado," Alec said excitedly.

I chuckled. "Can you call Kane and have him come home?"

Alec kissed me once more. "I'm on it."

He moved away from me and jogged out of the room with his phone pressed to his ear. I looked at Branna when she moved over to the large bag she left here a few weeks ago. Since she was my assigned midwife, it made sense for her to leave it here since I rarely left my apartment.

"Your liquid has a slight yellow tinge to it which is completely normal," Branna informed me. "I can see you're still leakin', but not by much. That puddle over there was an obvious gush so there won't be much left to leak out of you, but just to be safe I'll bring you inside to change. I want to put a pad on you to keep track of the colour of the water, okay? I'm going to be jottin' down notes on your form as I go along."

I nodded. "Okay, then what?"

"Then I'll check the baby's heartbeat and we can have a chat."

Check the baby's heartbeat and have a chat.

"Got it."

Branna and Nico both held onto me as I left the sitting room and entered my bedroom. Nico and Damien left and shut the door so I could undress and change.

"Can I shower?" I asked Branna.

She shook her head. "Wait another hour. I just want to watch your water to make sure there is no colour change."

I nodded my head. "Can you go wet a cloth then so I can wash down my legs, please?"

Branna bobbed her head up and down and then headed out of my room and into the bathroom. She returned with a warm, wet washcloth. She helped me strip naked and took the cloth and washed the lower half of my body.

I flushed. "I'm sorry you have to do this, I'm so embarrassed."

Branna snorted as she washed my thighs. "Babe, I help strangers do this on a daily basis at work. I'm happy to help you, you're one of me best friends."

I got emotional. "I'm so happy you're going to be deliverin' her."

Branna stood up when she was finished and leaned in, wrapping her arms around me. "Me too, sweetie. It is an honour."

When she separated, she got me a knee-length baby-blue nightie. She got a pair of granny knickers from one of the many new packets I bought for after the baby was born. She also grabbed one of my large pads and placed it onto the knickers then helped me slip them on.

I sighed. "I feel better knowing it will catch the water. It felt so weird when it just came out with no warnin'."

Branna smiled as we sat down on my bed. She asked me a few questions about my water breaking then she laid me back on my bed and went to get the little portable Doppler she had so she could check the baby's heartbeat.

When she returned to my room, Nico, Alec and Damien were hovering by the bedroom door looking in. I smiled at them and waved them in.

"Come in. I'm decent."

They entered the room but quickly made a show of looking up at the ceiling when Branna lifted my nightie upwards until it sat under my breasts. I chuckled at them and said, "I have big knickers on, lads. All you will see is belly and leg if you look."

They hesitantly peeked at me then fully looked when they saw I had nothing private on show. Alec climbed onto the bed and sat next to me while the twins stood a metre or two away from the bed, watching me warily.

"Where is Kane?" I asked Damien. "Is he on his way home?"

He licked his lips and said, "He didn't answer his phone, but we left text messages and voicemails. We'll keep on trying until he picks up."

I frowned. "He is with Ryder, why don't you try—"

"Already did." Nico cut me off. "He isn't answering either. They're both probably doing sets and their phones are on silent."

I blinked. "What if he misses the birth?"

Branna chuckled. "Darlin', this takes a while. Trust me, he will be here."

I nodded my head to Nico and said, "Did he take his injection this mornin'? I can't remember if he did or not."

"He took it," Alec confirmed. "He binned the needle in that yellow bucket on the kitchen counter when I came over."

I nodded my head and relaxed a little.

I glanced at Nico. "Did you ring Bronagh?"

"She and Keela are in town searching for a new bed since our base... broke."

I snorted. "You broke the base of your bed?"

He shrugged, smirking. "It was bound to happen at some point. I'm actually surprised it lasted so many years of us having sex on it *without* caving in."

I laughed.

My attention was brought to Branna when she squeezed some gel on my stomach. She turned on the little machine that found the baby's heartbeat, then placed the Doppler onto the gel on my stomach and swirled it around.

There was some static, then almost straight away there was a beautiful thudding sound.

I smiled, and so did Branna.

"The heartbeat is as strong as ever."

"Is it just me," Alec murmured, "or does the heartbeat sound scary similar to the beat of the song Jingle Bells?"

We laughed and listened for a minute more before she put the machine to the side and wiped my belly free of gel. We chatted then for a few more minutes, until everything stopped when a pain struck.

"Oh, shit," I winced and hunched forward, gripping onto my stomach as if it would somehow help ease the pain.

"Breathe," Branna's voice soothed. "Remember your breathing."

Right, my breathing.

Big inhale, long exhale, big inhale, long exhale.

I dropped my head back to my pillow when the pain eased. "Shit, that really hurts."

"That's labour, darlin'." Branna chuckled as she busied herself and grabbed different items from her bag, humming as she did so. There was a spring to her usual dragged step, and she looked happier than I'd seen her in a long time.

I hoped it was because of the baby coming and not because I was in pain because that's what the next four hours consisted of. Pain, pain, some laughter, and more fucking pain.

It was excruciating.

I had never felt anything like it before in my life, and there was no let-up to it either. I had some gas and sucked in air for pain relief, but even that only minimised it slightly by making me lightheaded.

Through my pain I noticed Kane still wasn't with me, and the more pain I felt, the more irritable I became about it. I needed him here, and he was nowhere to be found.

Damien even left at one point to go looking for him at the gym, but he came back alone and told me the manager said they left a few hours ago.

We had no clue where they were and all sorts of horrible things ran through my mind. Things like what if Big Phil somehow had him?

I tried not to think about it as the contractions came faster, and lasted longer. The entire time Branna was monitoring the baby's heartbeat, which always remained strong and steady like it was supposed to. She checked to see how far along I was dilated every thirty minutes to an hour, and during the last hour I went from five centimetres to ten. The brothers had set up the birthing pool Kane and I purchased weeks ago, in our bedroom, and Branna lit some candles and played soft, instrumental music.

It really helped me relax, or relax as much as could.

I was in the middle of pulling my nightie off my body and fanning myself as heat attacked every inch of my body. I was naked from the waist down, but I didn't care. I had a comfortable sports bra on, but nothing else.

I was too far gone with pain to even consider the brothers being uncomfortable. I didn't care about them or anyone else; I just cared about myself and my own comfort.

"Fuck, fuck, fuucccckkkk," I all but snarled as I bent forward and placed my hands on my bed. I swayed from side to side and tried to focus on the music instead of the pain that stabbed me.

"Branna," I said in a very calm voice when the urge to get this baby out of my body occurred. "I need to push. I need to push right *now*."

Branna and the lads lead me to the birthing pool.

"This is very different than what I imagined seeing Aideen's private parts would be like," Alec murmured from behind me as I eased myself down into the birthing pool.

Nico choked on air. "You imagined that? Bro, she is our brother's girl. The mother to our *niece* or *nephew*."

I looked up at them when I was settled on my knees and leaning on the pool's side.

Alec blinked. "I've imagined it since I first met her... should I be sorry about that? Because I'm not."

Nico shook his head. "I'm telling Kane you said that."

"You've always been a little snitch bitch!" Alec hissed.

"Time and place, bro," Damien grumbled. "Time and place."

I wanted to laugh at them; they sounded like arguing little boys, but I couldn't because all I could focus on was the pain that consumed me.

"Kane!" I cried as a mighty contraction tore through me. "Oh, please. I need him."

"Death!" Alec hissed. "That is what he has asked for by not answering his fucking phone!"

Nico nodded in agreement then reached for my hand and grabbed ahold of it.

"He will be here, Ado."

"When?" I screamed and squeezed Nico's hand when the pain I felt intensified. "I'm goin' to fuckin' *kill* him if he isn't already dead or worse."

Nico's face turned red and his eyes almost bugged out of their sockets.

"Ow," he whimpered. "Ow. Ow. That hurts."

I let go of his hands and focused on Alec laughing at Nico as he shook out his hand and cradled it against his chest.

"I can't do this," I panted.

Branna looked up and locked her eyes on mine. "Babe, a few more minutes and you'll be a mammy. You got this."

I didn't have anything.

I couldn't fucking do it.

"Make it stop," I screamed as burning filled my vagina. "Help it stop. Damien!"

"Oh Christ," he whispered and scrambled closer to me, but full blown panic came over him and he could do nothing but move to the side and rub my hand.

Alec took his place in front of me.

"Take her mind off of it," Nico whispered to him, but had his eyes locked between my legs.

The way I was positioned was not ladylike at all.

"Sons of Anarchy!" Alec suddenly shouted. "I'll put on the show and you can-"

"Shut. Up," I growled as I stared at him. "And don't move a bloody muscle. You're me focus point."

He began to panic and started to sing, "I love you, you love me. We're a happy family-"

"Alec!" Nico snapped. "Barney songs? Really?"

Alec placed his hands on the side of his head and he whimpered, "I don't know what to do!"

"Just do what Aideen asks," Branna said in a calm voice as she dabbed a cool damp cloth over my forehead.

Alec looked at Branna then to me then to Nico. "I take it back. I don't want babies, not ever."

"Bronagh is already pregnant," Dominic cried into his hands. "It's too late to pull out."

"I'm never ever having sex ever again," Damien whispered.

For God's sake.

"Stop pushing?" Alec then suggested. "Squeeze your cheeks together and keep that little Slater up there until Kane gets here."

Branna and Nico looked at Alec who was demonstrating to me what I had to do with my arse cheeks. I didn't want to copy him because he looked constipated and it freaked me out.

"It doesn't work like that, Alec," Branna said then refocused on me and smiled. "Honey, you're doing beautifully."

"She can't do beautifully because Kane isn't here!" Alec stated for a second time. "He needs to be here for this."

Branna laughed. "Tell the baby that."

Alec did just that. The bloody freak of nature kneeled down next to the pool, cupped his hands at the sides of his mouth and shouted, "Stop your journey down the vaginal canal, we're not ready for you yet. Your daddy is at the gym pumping iron, have some respect and wait for him!"

Dominic pulled Alec away from my most private body part and smacked him on the nose. "Stop it."

Alec jumped with fright and silently lifted his fingers to his nose while he stared at his brother with wide eyes.

"I can't believe you just did that to me."

Nico shook his head, chewing on his inner cheek probably so he wouldn't smile. Branna rubbed Alec's shoulder, smiling before she looked back to me and winked.

"Aideen?!"

Oh, thank God.

Branna smiled wide. "In the bedroom!"

Seconds passed by, then Kane and Ryder burst into the bedroom. I didn't look up. Instead, I lowered my head and screamed as pain swam around my abdomen.

"Strip down and get into the pool with her, she needs you," Branna ordered Kane.

"Where the fuck have you been?" I screamed as I pushed.

I ignored everything and picked up the two balls Branna had given me earlier and continued to squeeze and release them in my hands, focusing all the pain I felt into the objects.

And breathing, I really needed to remember my breathing.

I heard mindless chatter and sounds of items hitting my bedroom floor, then I heard water splashing, as ripples of water knocked against me.

Kane was in the pool.

I felt a hand pressed against my back, then multiple kisses to my shoulder.

"I'm here, babydoll."

I began to cry, the relief of having him here hit me like a bomb. I was terrified he would miss the baby being born.

"I'm sorry," he whispered and kissed the side of my head. "I'm so sorry."

I turned my head to him, pressing it to the side of his face. "I can't do this."

Kane smiled. "What are you talking about? You're doing it, and you're doing it fucking awesomely."

"Hell yeah she is," Branna agreed.

Kane interlocked his hands with mine and didn't make a sound when I squeezed him with every ounce of energy I had.

"God, it hurts!" I cried out and held our conjoined hands under my stomach.

"Spread your legs as wide as you can, honey, and as soon as your get another contraction you bear down and push, okay?"

I nodded to Branna and gripped Kane's hands as Branna instructed me to move our affixed hands under my thighs as I pushed. It didn't take long for a contraction to hit, and when it did, I did what Branna had said and I pushed. Contractions were painful and just utterly horrid, but pushing?

Pushing. Hurt. Like. Hell.

I screamed as loud as I ever had in my life when burning ripped through my vagina. "*Ahhhhhhh!*" I roared until my contraction faded, but even then the burning lingered.

"Branna," I cried and squeeze my eyes shut. "It's burnin'."

I felt the cloth against my head.

"Push through that sting, do you hear me? You push through it with everythin' you've got."

I did just that. For thirty more minutes I pushed like hell through the burning sting until I thought I would collapse from exhaustion.

"She's crownin', that means the head is almost out, Kane," Branna whispered. "You're about to deliver your baby."

Fear struck me.

"Branna, help him," I pleaded, terrified Kane might let the baby fall by mistake.

"I'm ready," he breathed. "I've got this, babydoll, trust me. Push as hard as you can one more time."

Ryder and his brothers hunkered down in front of me and they each grabbed my hands, arms and legs, letting me use them as leverage.

"Let's do this, Ado." Alec smiled.

I nodded my head, then I sucked in a huge breath and with all my might, I bore down and pushed like my life depended on it.

"Good girl, babydoll," Kane cheered. "Keep pushing... keep pushing."

"The head is fully out," Branna whooped a few seconds later.

More burning pain flooded my vagina and I screamed, but quickly inhaled and exhaled through the pain.

Nico moved to the side to get a better view and laughed. "Nothing but dark hair, a true Slater." He tried to high five Damien who pointed at his own mop of white hair causing Nico to wince and say, "My bad, bro."

I screamed loudly once more as increasing pressure mounted at my entrance, intensifying the burning.

Kane was laughing as he said, "Shoulders are out... chest... torso... butt... legs... and toes. You *did* it, baby."

I slumped forward as I felt the baby leave me.

"It's a... *boy!*" Kane suddenly announced. "It's *definitely* a boy."

I gasped and tried to look down between my legs, but the water was clouded with blood. "Are you sure?"

Branna carefully sat me back and leaned over into the pool and lifted my leg so Kane could wind the umbilical cord under so I didn't hurt myself or the baby. I turned my head and burst into tears as I looked at Kane who had our baby scooped up in his big arms. I was smiling and weeping until I noticed something.

The baby wasn't crying.

"Branna," I said. "Why isn't he cryin'?"

"It's normal, give him a second," Branna said then reached over and took the baby from Kane without asking.

He still wasn't crying.

Five-seconds of nothing passed and it felt like a lifetime.

"Oh, please," I screamed as panic struck. "Please make him

cry."

Kane grabbed hold of my shoulders as I tried to stand up. I shoved him away from me and tried to make it closer to Branna. She couldn't move very far because the baby's umbilical cord was still attached to me.

"Come on, baby boy," Branna cooed to the baby as she rubbed him roughly with one of our baby towels. She continued this while I wailed and Kane hugged me from behind.

Alec had his hands on either side of his head, Nico and Damien were both chewing on their nails, and Ryder was just staring at the baby and Branna.

Time was frozen until... magic.

The loudest wail you could imagine from a newborn filled my apartment, and it was the best sound I had ever heard in my entire life.

I cried harder with relief that the baby was alive, and Kane, who was shaking behind me, whimpered lightly and pressed his face into the back of my hair.

"You little brat," Branna tearfully laughed as she finished wiping the baby's face. "Givin' your mammy and daddy a fright like that."

"Your fuckin' uncles, too," Alec stated and bent forward, placing his hands on his knees, panting like he just ran a marathon.

Branna moved over to us and leaned down. She lowered her arms, and gently rested the baby onto my chest. I scanned my eyes over the baby until my eyes rested in between *his* legs.

"It *is* a boy," I cried with happiness. "We have a son."

Kane wrapped his arms around us and kissed the side of my face. "Thank you so much, baby."

"For what?" I sniffled, looking back to him.

"For giving him to me," he said and kissed my lips.

I cried with happiness and looked back down to my son who started to cry, loudly. "Shhh," I cooed and gently rocked him. "Mammy's got you."

My heart burst with love in that moment.

I was someone's mother.

"He looks just like you, Kane," Branna commented through her soft crying.

"No way," he murmured, his eyes locked on our child's face. "He's beautiful, that's all Aideen."

I smiled with glee, and let my eyes roam over my son's face. He had a cute button nose, real chubby cheeks, a head full of dark brown hair and plump pink lips. I lifted him up and leaned my mouth down to his head and I kissed him.

"I love you," I whispered. "I love you *so* much, baby boy."

Kane repositioned himself behind me. He put his legs on either side of my hips and pulled me and our baby back into his chest. He leaned his head into the side of mine and we both stared down at out little angel.

"I can't believe we made him," I murmured. "He is perfect."

"He is," Kane agreed.

Branna reached down and gently pressed on my breast and the baby gurgled then hummed as he relaxed even more against me. I closed my eyes as she moved to her bag and took some objects out. I felt her come back over and lean over me and the baby, but I only opened my eyes when she spoke to Kane.

"Cut between the clamp and my fingers."

I opened my eyes and saw Branna handing Kane a funny shaped pair of scissors and then glanced down to the baby's umbilical cord. What I can only describe as a white peg was clamped near the baby's belly button and Branna was directing Kane where to cut.

Kane did as told and cut through our son's umbilical cord. It took a few cuts, but he cut it off and handed Branna back her scissors.

"You might want to claw my eyes out, but can I have him for a few minutes? I'll dry him off and wrap him up nice and warm."

I frowned at Branna. "Why?"

Branna chuckled. "I have to help you deliver the placenta, babe, and I want to weigh him."

Oh, right.

"Okay," I glowered and carefully handed my son over to her.

Branna smiled as she leaned in and kissed my head. "He will be back in your arms before you know it."

I hoped so, I already missed him.

Branna weighed the baby, and he was ten pounds on the dot.

Ten. Fucking. Pounds.

I was terrified to think how big he would have grown had I carried him full-term.

After weighing him, Branna then cleaned him up and placed him in the Moses basket next to my bed. Everyone, except Kane, left the room then as Branna came to my side.

The next ten minutes were painful, but not as painful as active labour.

"There you go," Branna said as she pressed on my stomach once more.

I winced as I felt something pass through my body.

"All done," Branna announced then reached into the water and lifted a clump of something nasty looking and placed it into a plastic bag next to her.

Branna lifted our son from the Moses basket and gave him back to me, I held my arms up making sure the blanket he was wrapped in didn't touch the water of the pool.

I glanced up when I heard a soft click. I noticed Branna had left the room so it was just Kane, our son and me.

"I was so scared there for a second."

Kane kissed my shoulder. "Me too, sweetheart. My heart stopped."

Mine did, too.

Our son wailed and it made me chuckle when Kane said, "I love your cry."

I gazed at him then murmured to him, "You don't think the smoke from that night hurt him, right?"

"No," Kane replied. "Look at him; he is healthy as can be. Pink and big all over."

His little face was pressed against my chest, and his instinct took over. He tried to suckle on my skin so I nervously repositioned him under my breast as I remembered what Branna had taught me. Kane reached around and adjusted my breast and nipple with his hand until it was close to the baby's mouth.

It took about a minute of adjusting, and brushing my nipple against our son's mouth, but he eventually latched on and began to suckle.

"Ow," I winced.

"Are you okay?" Kane asked me, his voice barely a whisper.

I nodded, but continued to wince. "It hurts a little, but it's okay. Branna said that a little pain was normal."

Kane pressed his face to the side of mine, and we both looked down as our son fed for the first time. I heard a little click, but didn't look up. I heard some movement then the sound of a shutter caught my attention.

I looked up and saw Branna smiling apologetically as she tucked her phone into her trouser pocket.

"Sorry, it was too perfect of a moment not to capture."

I smiled and looked back down to my son.

"How is everythin'?" Branna's voice whispered.

"Perfect."

"Branna," Kane murmured. "He latched on."

"Brilliant," she beamed as she moved closer. "Are you feelin' okay, Aideen?"

I nodded my head.

I felt incredible.

I looked down to the baby when the pressure on my nipple lessened. I noticed he unlatched and smacked his lips together a few times, before just lying in my arms in a baby drunk daze.

"Your colostrum must taste good," Kane chuckled. "Look at him."

I smiled. "I love him so much."

"Me too, babydoll."

"Put him in his Moses basket," Branna instructed, "and we'll get her out of the pool. I want her dried and into warm clothes as soon as possible. I don't want her to catch a bug; she's very vulnerable right now."

Kane sprang into action as he climbed out of the birthing pool.

He very carefully placed our son in his Moses basket that was by my side of the bed. He came for me then, and with Branna's help, they got me up and out of the birthing pool. I walked slowly away from the pool and winced. I could move, but it hurt to do so.

Branna went and got a basin of hot water and both she and Kane washed me down with a sponge bath. It only took a minute, but I felt so refreshed after and relaxed into Kane as he wrapped a large towel around me and rubbed me dry.

He dried himself off and changed clothes in record time. When I was completely dried off, Branna checked my privates once more and said she was very pleased that I had no tear from delivery. When she gave me the go-ahead, I stepped into a large pair of granny knickers that had the mother of all maxi pads attached to it. After that was up, I got into a new fresh pair of loose pyjamas. Kane gave me a bobbin and held onto my hips as I tied my hair up into a bun that sat on top of my head.

I needed to wash it and take a proper shower, since I never got the one I wanted during the early stage of my labour, but that could wait until tomorrow. Right now, I was clean and totally exhausted. I needed to get into my bed, which Kane helped me with since it wasn't low to the floor. When I climbed under my covers, I winced a little then glanced at the clock on the wall and saw it was half seven in the evening.

I couldn't believe it; it felt like the day was never ending, and it was only half seven. That meant I had only been in labour for seven hours. It seemed like a long time, but I knew from research, and Branna, that it was considered a quick birth especially for a first time mother.

"Are you up for some visitors?" Kane asked me.

I blinked. "Who's here?"

He snorted. "Your father, all your brothers, all my brothers and all of the girls."

I smiled and nodded my head. "Of course they can come in. They've waited to see him as long as we have."

Kane left the room to get them as Branna picked up my son from his Moses basket and placed him in my arms. Branna had put a blue baby hat on his head to lock the heat in. He was wrapped up tightly in a thick blanket, cocooning him.

"He isn't dressed."

I blinked. "Could you do it? I want to watch you so I can copy. I fear I will hurt him."

Branna smiled as she took my sleeping son and laid him across the bed. "I gave him a quick wash like I did you, but you can give him his first proper bath tomorrow after you get some rest."

I nodded my head and watched as she unravelled the blanket from my son. I found myself leaning over to check between his legs.

I smiled when Branna laughed. "I'm just checkin' to make sure he is really a boy... I can't believe it. I thought for sure he was a girl."

"Kane and all the brothers were right, that's a bloody first," she chuckled.

I didn't look up when the door to my bedroom opened; I was too focused on what Branna was doing. She was carefully putting the tiniest nappy onto my son, mindful of the clamp on his umbilical cord.

"Omigod," I heard a female whisper.

I felt people enter the room, but I couldn't look away from Branna's hands as she dressed my son. She gently put a vest on him followed by a blue baby grown, mittens and a white cardigan. She adjusted his hat and I smiled when he yawned and made a squealing noise.

Branna lifted him up, kissed his cheek then placed him in my arms. I looked up then and smiled. Everyone was in my room, and they all had huge smiles on their faces. There were some tears, too.

"Aideen," Keela blubbered and came to my side of the bed.

She leaned in, kissed my cheek. "Well done, honey."

I smiled in thanks and looked down to my son when she placed her hand on his little arm.

"He is perfect," she whispered.

I agreed wholeheartedly.

"Darlin'."

I looked up and smiled wide. "Hey, Granda."

My father's resolve broke as tears fell from his eyes. Keela moved over to her place in front of Alec while my father sat next to me on my bed and put an arm around my shoulders. He kissed my face and hugged me to him before we both gazed down at my bundle of joy.

"He looks just like you," my father murmured. "So beautiful."

I smiled again and lifted my arms. "Do you want to hold him?"

My father nodded his head and stood up. He reached down, and gently picked up his grandson, holding him protectively against his chest. Tears welled up in my eyes as I watched him interact with my baby.

He cooed down at him when he whimpered a little and swayed from side to side.

"Hey, buddy," he whispered. "I'm your Granda."

That was it.

My tears came fast and furious, making a few of the lads laugh.

"Well done, baby sister."

I smiled at James when he came over to hug me, followed by my other brothers. Gavin held onto me the longest and told me loved me more than anything in the world... except his nephew. That made me chuckle.

"What is his name?" This came from Bronagh.

I looked to Kane who looked as lost as I felt.

"No idea yet."

Everyone chuckled at us.

I hugged Kane's brothers then, and I thanked and apologised to Nico, Alec and Damien for any harm or discomfort I brought to them during my labour. They smiled at me and waved it off like it was no big deal.

I cried some more when I got to the girls. They all cried, even Alannah who was usually the best of us for controlling her emotions. We all laughed and chatted as my son was passed around to everyone. I watched as each and every one of them fell in love with my child, and it only caused my love for *them* to grow.

I don't know how long everyone stayed, but by the time everyone left, even Branna after she checked on us both once more, I was close to falling asleep sitting up. I had just finished feeding the baby again and settled back into my bed when a switch flipped inside of me.

It was an odd sequence of events. One moment I was so captivated by my newborn son, that I forgot about everything, and the next the mist of joy that clouded my mind lifted and confusion set in.

I looked at Kane and frowned.

I didn't think much of it earlier because I was in labour, and afterwards it never occurred to me because I was so wrapped up in the baby and everyone else... but now that I had a minute to think, I was curious to know where Kane had been all day.

I was curious to know why he almost missed our son's birth.

"Kane?"

He was folding up the birthing pool.

"Hmmm?"

I tiredly blinked. "Where were you all day today?"

He froze.

His hesitation in answering caused my stomach to churn.

"Kane?" I whispered.

The muscles on his back contracted.

"What?" he asked after a moment of silence.

He knew what I asked, but he was stalling.

"Alec was calling you for ages, Ryder too, but neither of you answered. Where were you?"

"I was in the gym for about two hours," he replied.

I swallowed. "And for the other hours?"

He placed the birthing pool back into its container then turned to face me.

"Helping Ryder move... some stuff."

Tears welled in my eyes.

"Kane."

He took a step forward. "I swear if I knew you would be having the baby today I wouldn't have left your side."

I held my hand up in the air. "Stay where you are."

Kane tensed, but nodded.

I lowered my hand to my stomach and exhaled. "You were movin' drugs or weapons... weren't you?"

Kane opened his mouth, but closed it when no words came out. I watched his hands ball into fists just as I felt the tears that welled up in my eyes spill onto my cheeks.

"Please let me come to you."

I shook my head. "I was in labour all day... and you were out helpin' Ryder with that horrible stuff."

Kane swallowed. "I'm—"

"Your *brothers* held my hands, listened to me scream and curse at them, and did everythin' in their power to help me. They never left me side the entire time. They were scared shitless, but they were there for me."

"Aideen," Kane whispered, his own eyes glazing with unshed tears.

"You almost missed him comin' into this world."

Kane couldn't hold my gaze anymore. He dropped his head and sagged his shoulders in shame.

"I'm disgusted with myself for not being here for it all."

I was disgusted with him too.

"What did I tell you?" I asked him.

He looked up at me and shrugged.

"I told you I wouldn't be with you when you're attached to that life."

Pure panic marred Kane's features.

"Please," he begged in a low voice. "Please forgive me. I won't do it again. I won't help Ryder ever again. I swear on my life."

It hurt me seeing him so desperate, but I decided I had to be cruel to be kind. I loved him, and I was *not* letting our relationship fail because of his stupid mistakes. He was my forever, and I was going to make him realise the baby and myself were *his*.

I kept my expression as blank as I possibly could; I tried my hardest to be heartless.

I was about to scare him straight.

"I think you should leave," I said, locking my gaze with his.

"Aideen," he choked and stumbled forward until his knees knocked into our bed. "Please, I'm begging you, *don't* do this."

Don't break until he does.

"I didn't do anythin', *you* did," I replied leisurely. "I've asked you, no I've *begged* you, repeatedly, to tell me what you and Ryder were up to, and I've pleaded with you not to be involved with it... but you completely ignored me. You said it wouldn't take you from me, but it has. You almost missed the birth of your son for it... was it worth it?"

"I'm so sorry," he croaked, as tears fell from his eyes and dropped onto his cheeks.

Put the fear of God into him.

"No, *I'm* sorry, Kane," I said with a shake of my head. "I'm sorry I let this go so far. I truly thought your love and respect for me would be enough for you to do the right thing, but I'm obviously not worth it. You chose somethin' dangerous, illegal and plain *disgustin'* over me."

I looked down to my left hand, wiggled the engagement ring off my finger and threw it to the end of the bed where it landed before him. He looked at me with widened eyes and the look of utter heartbreak that encased him was almost too much for me to bear. But I needed him to realise that he could lose me over something he thought wasn't much of a problem.

I wanted him scared shitless.

"Please don't leave me," he cried. "I'd die without you."

I looked to our son so he wouldn't see my act was falling apart.

"If you don't put me first, what's to say you won't put him first?"

I looked back to Kane as he grabbed my engagement ring and crawled up the bed until he was face to face with me.

"I'm begging you not to do this. You and that precious boy are my everything, I swear to you."

I frowned. "I don't know if that's enough for us to work."

"Babydoll," he breathed and placed his hands on my cheeks. "I'm willing to do whatever it takes to make this work. I don't want to lose what I live for. You and our son. I never thought it was possible to love two people as much as I do you two. I love you both so much it hurts. Please, don't take away my reason for living."

Damn him!

I leaned into him. "You swear on *his* life that you're done with anything related to your old life?"

"I swear." He frantically nodded. "I swear to God."

I regarded him for a long moment before I nodded and said, "Okay."

Kane crumbled before me, and pressed his forehead against mine. I forced myself not to fall apart, but my God it was hard. I had never seen him so broken, and it gutted me that I caused it, but I *had* to.

I had to scare him into believing I was really done with him; if I hadn't, who knows how long he would have 'helped' Ryder for. For all I knew, it probably would have forced us apart in the long run and broken our family.

"I love you so fucking much," he whispered.

I put my arms around his neck. "I love you too, sweetheart... now give me my ring back."

Kane wiped his face before he placed the ring back on my finger and kissed it. I lifted my hand and nudged his head up until he was looking at me.

"You have me heart," I told him. "Don't *ever* forget that."

He nodded his head. "I won't, not ever."

I kissed him then, and he kissed me back with a fierce hunger. It lasted a few moments before he pulled back and rustled around until he was under the bed cover next to me.

"Lie down," he urged. "I need to hold you."

He helped me get settled on the bed before he stretched out next to me.

"Babydoll?"

I snuggled back against him and murmured, "Yes."

"I say it all the time, but I really do love you with all of my heart. You know that, right?"

I closed my eyes and smiled. "I know, babe. I'm sorry about being so horrible, I never want to hurt you or make you cry."

"You had every right to be furious with me. I almost missed our son being born over Ryder and his stupid deals."

I snuggled into my pillow. "Let's not talk about it anymore. It's done now and your decision has been made. You made it for his birth and that's all that matters."

I felt Kane nod as he hugged me, lowering his hands down to my stomach.

"It's all flabby," I grumbled.

Kane snorted. "It's weird that your stomach isn't huge and hard. I can still feel a smaller bump, but Branna said that will go down in a few days as your womb starts the process of shrinking back to normal."

I looked over my shoulder. "You talked to her about stuff like that?"

"All the time," he nodded. "I want to know what you're going through."

I smiled and looked forward, staring into our son's Moses basket.

"What will we name him?" I questioned.

Kane sighed. "I don't know, what do you like?"

I grinned. "Promise you won't laugh?" Kane nodded his head so I said, "Jax."

He broke his promise and laughed, lowly.

"Hey."

"Sorry," he chuckled.

I frowned. "You don't like it."

"I actually do. I was just thinking of how Jax Teller brought us together that fateful day in Ryder and Branna's house."

I grinned. "Through Jax Teller all things are possible."

Kane chuckled. "Jax Slater... that sounds cool."

"Jax Slater," I repeated. "I love it."

"So we're settled on his name being Jax?"

I nodded with excitement and said, "Yeah, but what will his middle name be?"

"I was thinking of his middle name being after your dad."

I felt my lower lip wobble. "Really?"

"Of course," Kane nodded. "Your dad is awesome, and the look of admiration and love he holds for you and Jax fills my heart. He is a good man, and will be an awesome papaw."

I beamed. "Papaw. That's so cute, I love that."

Kane chuckled. "So his name is Jax Daniel Slater?"

"Yes! Wait, Jax Daniel... sounds like Jack Daniels."

Kane burst into laughter. "We can't change it now, we already agreed."

Oh, man.

I lightly laughed. "Me da will get a right kick out of this."

"I love you, Jax," Kane murmured after out laughter subsided.

I placed my hands on top of his and said, "Me and you?"

"Me and you."

I smiled then and closed my eyes as sleep grabbed me. The last thing I remembered before I fell into darkness was that my heart was even fuller as another Slater man entered my life and dominated it.

CHAPTER EIGHT

Twelve weeks later...

It was the ever familiar sound that made a tired mother sigh, and a new uncle reel in horror.

"*Please* don't tell me you just did that, Jax."

Jax farted for a second time, and the follow through was louder than before.

"Oh, my God!" Nico gasped then heaved when the foul smell reached his nostrils. "Quick, take him."

I laughed at Jax's grinning face, and Nico's revolted one.

"No."

Nico looked at me with wide, horrified eyes. "What do you mean, *no*? He needs his diaper changed! He stinks."

I stayed seated. "*You're* goin' to change him."

"Me?!" Nico screeched.

He looked terrified.

I calmly nodded my head. "You need to practice. Bronagh will have your baby before you know it. Nappy changin' is a skill you need to master sooner rather than later."

Nico looked visibly ill.

"What if I hurt him? He is *tiny*."

I deadpanned. "You got away with that excuse when he was a

newborn, but he is twelve weeks old now; he is much bigger and sturdier. You won't break him."

"But—"

"You're changin' him."

Nico groaned in defeat and looked at Jax. "I love you, little man, but I don't love the presents you leave in your diapers."

I snorted. "Get used to it; you have all this ahead of you."

Nico grumbled to himself as he stood up with Jax in his arms and walked towards the sitting room door. He paused at the doorway and looked over to me and said, "I need you to instruct me on what to do. Come with me."

I chuckled as I stood up and followed him out of the sitting room, and down to Jax's bedroom. I leaned against the doorframe of the room and watched as Nico lays my son down on top of his changing table.

"What do I do first?" Nico asked, not taking his eyes away from Jax.

"Take off his babygrow and vest. Open the nappy he is wearin', roll it up with one hand and put it into the bin bag on the side of the table. Before you do that though, pull out some baby wipes so you can grab them quickly to avoid a mess. A fresh nappy is to your right. When he is wiped and powdered, you put it on. Easy."

"Easy? Missions to space take less fucking instructions from NASA than that!"

I burst into laughter.

"Are you okay?" I quickly asked when he dry heaved again.

Nico composed himself and nodded his head. "We got this, haven't we, buddy?" he cooed to Jax.

Jax had his fingers in his mouth and was busy chewing on them, but when Nico spoke to him, he gave his uncle his undivided attention. He began to talk in his baby language, and it melted my heart.

"He does this with you, your brothers and *my* brothers all the time! He smiles and tries to talk, but with the girls he doesn't have the time of day for them. He just grabs at them."

Nico didn't look up from unbuttoning Jax's babygrow as he said, "He's a Slater, it's wired into him to choose bros over hoes."

I snickered. "I'm tellin' the girls you called them hoes."

"I'll deny it," Nico said, grinning to himself.

I snorted and watched as Nico stripped Jax of his baby grow and vest. He did a good job in taking them off gently. He was about to open the wings of the nappy, but just as he was about to do it my apartment door opened.

I leaned backwards and looked to see who it was. I saw an arm and a colourful dragon tattoo that told me who my visitor was.

"Hey, Alec."

Alec stepped into my apartment and closed the door after himself. He looked in my direction after hearing my greeting. He smiled and walked down the hallway to me.

"Hey, preggers."

I deadpanned. "I told you not to call me that until I begin to show again."

"Sorry, I forgot."

I playfully rolled my eyes then screeched when Alec poked my sides.

"I can't believe you're six weeks pregnant," he said in awe. "The first time you and Kane have sex after Jax is born and he knocks you up. His dick is lethal."

I laughed. "It was a build-up of no sex for six weeks ... he just got excited."

"I'll say." Alec laughed.

I shook my head, chuckling. "We wanted to try again anyway, so it worked out."

"Is Dominic still here?" he then asked.

I nodded. "He's in here."

I leaned my shoulder back against the doorframe and snorted when Alec came up behind me so he could see into Jax's room.

He said, "What the fuck is he doing?"

Nico still had his fingertips on the wings of the nappy, but he hesitated in pulling them open.

"Changin' his first nappy," I answered Alec.

He grunted in distaste. "*Why?*"

"Because Bronagh is pregnant. He needs to learn."

Alec huffed. "What's there to learn? You take off the dirty diaper, wipe and powder, and then put on a fresh one. I watch Teen Mom, I know what I'm talking about."

"It's not that easy!" Nico hissed without taking his eyes away from Jax and his nappy.

Alec snorted. "Sure it is."

"Help me then," Nico challenged.

"I got this," Alec said and slid past me into Jax's room.

Alec moved over to Nico's side and looked down at his nephew.

"My little man!" he gushed. "You're so cute—oh Jesus! What *is* that smell?"

Nico grunted and covered his nose with his hand. "It's Jax."

"Oh, bro," Alec whispered and plugged his nostrils with his fingers. "That is not right, should he smell like that? He might have a disease."

Nico gasped and girly slapped Alec's shoulder. "Don't say that!"

I was holding onto my side because a stitch developed from laughing.

"He is fine," I panted, "that's just a normal smell."

Alec scrunched up his face in disgust. "It smells like something crawled up inside his ass and died."

"Stop it!" I cackled.

Alec shook his head as he looked down at my son. "You out stink Storm, buddy. That's *not* cool."

Jax was still chewing on his fingers as he laughed up at Alec and began to talk to him. Jax was having a full on conversation and Alec responded with head nods and funny questions.

Nico smiled at Jax. "Who do you like better, me or this chump?" He jabbed his thumb at Alec.

Jax grumbled a few sounds but it in all honesty, it really sounded like there was a 'lec' sound in his baby sentence, which, of course, made Alec scream with joy.

"He. Said. Alec!"

Nico rolled his eyes. "He did not, he was blowing spit bubbles."

"He did, too. He said my name. I'm his favourite," Alec proudly announced. "Good choice, my little man."

Nico shook his head at his brother. Alec grinned back at Nico. "When Bronagh has your baby, I'm gonna be the favourite with him, too."

"I doubt that."

"Never doubt the baby whisperer."

The baby whisperer?

I slapped my hands on my knees as I cried with laughter. Nico and Alec were hilarious when separate, but together they were too much for me to deal with.

"Okay, *baby whisperer*," Nico challenged. "You go get the butt powder while I take off his diaper."

"I got this," Alec replied with a firm nod of his head.

He looked at me and asked, "Where is the powder?"

I pointed to the bookcase that we converted into a holder for all of the things needed to clean up Jax. I had a few different powders for Alec to choose from, and I saw him tense up when he stood in front of the case and stared at them all.

"Alec!" Nico heaved. "Hurry!"

I looked to Nico and saw he got Jax's nappy off and was currently dropping it into the bin bag on the side of the table like it was a live grenade. He grabbed a handful of the wipes, as in *way* too many, and quickly began to clean his behind and privates.

"It's under his balls!" he cried out in dismay.

I covered my mouth with my hand to muffle down my laughter.

"I'm sorry to have to clean you here, bro," Nico said to Jax who laughed up at him.

Nico shook his head. "You're enjoying this aren't you? You little fart."

Jax clapped his hands together and it made Nico laugh. When he finished cleaning Jax up, Nico looked over his shoulder to his brother and shook his head. "What's the matter, baby whisperer? Are you having trouble with the butt powder?"

"No!" Alec instantly replied. "I'm just trying to make a decision."

"Well, hurry up."

I began to howl with laughter when Alec fumbled with nerves as he looked for the baby powder. He was jumping back and forth from one foot to the other as if it would help him complete his task quicker.

"Alec!" Nico snapped. "Give me the damn powder! He doesn't want to lie down anymore. Hurry!"

"Don't rush me!" Alec shouted as he quickly scanned his eyes over the labels on the baby products.

"Ah-ha!" he whooped. "I found it. This is the one Kane uses on him!"

Nico growled. "Open it and give it here then!"

Alec turned and looked down to the baby powder. He gripped the body of the bottle with one hand and used his other hand to turn the cap.

Don't squeeze the bottle!

I tried to flag him down and warn him of the impending danger, but it was too late. Alec opened the powder, and the pressure on the body of the bottle from his grip caused white powder to shoot from the top of the bottle directly into his face.

For a second everything stopped and, in slow motion, a cloud of white smoke consumed Alec's head and upper body, but when I realised what just happened, I admit I wet myself a tiny bit.

I fell against the door frame as my laughter turned to wheezing. I crossed my legs to stop myself from having a full on accident and fanned my face when I felt like it was overheating.

"Are you fucking kidding me!?" Alec shouted, then sputtered as the powder got in his mouth.

"Don't cuss!" Nico snapped.

Alec rubbed powder out of his eyes then reached out and smacked the back of Nico's head. "Look at me! Don't tell me not to fucking cuss!"

Nico bent his leg and tried to kick Alec with a backward strike. "If I didn't have this baby on this table, I'd kick your ass!"

Oh, God, *please*.

I was going to have a heart attack from laughing. I watched through blurred eyes as Nico lifted Jax from his changing table and placed him into his playpen so he could take Alec on.

"Stop," I begged.

"This is *not* funny, Aideen!" Alec bellowed at me. "I look like Tony from Scarface after he dove head first into a pile of cocaine."

That was it.

I was done.

I sunk down to the floor and cried with both laughter and pain from the horrendous stitch in my side.

"She's down!" Alec screeched and rushed over to me.

I sputtered and coughed.

"Is it the baby?" Alec asked in a panic as he kneeled next to me and placed his powdered hands on my stomach.

"No," I wheezed. "It's you two. So... funny!"

Alec hissed in disgust. "I thought you were hurt you bitch! Don't scare me like that again."

I continued to laugh. "I love you so much."

Alec rolled his eyes. "Stop professing your love for me. I'm *not* having sex with you, get over it already."

I slapped at Alec's chest and shoulders as tears of laughter streamed down my face.

He was too much.

I lay back on the floor and laughed.

I couldn't hear anything over my own laughter until footsteps vibrated on the floorboards under me. I opened my eyes and through the blur of my laughing tears I saw my one and only.

"Kane," I cackled.

He tilted his head as he looked down at me. "Are you okay?" he asked with a smile on his face.

"I'm perfect," I said and wiped my tear-streaked face.

He shook his head at me. "Babydoll, why are you on the floor crying with laughter? And what's with all the powder?"

I couldn't form a sentence to answer his question so I pointed into Jax's room. Kane turned his head and looked into the room and within seconds his eyes widened. "What... what the ever loving fuck happened in here?"

"*They* happened!" I howled.

I lifted my head and saw that Alec and Nico were tussling, and they were both covered in the baby powder now, not just Alec. They both stopped and began to stand up when they saw Kane. It was short lived as Alec muttered something to Nico that caused Nico to flip out and jump back on Alec who dropped like a ton of bricks when the weight of Nico's body pressed down on him.

Kane didn't move a muscle; he simply shook his head and looked away from his brothers who were rolling around the white powdered floor like toddlers wrestling. His eyes refocused on me and he grinned. "You want a hand up?"

"I don't think I can stand, I've laughed myself into paralysis."

Kane snickered and reached down where he hooked his hands under my arms and pulled. One second I was on the floor, and the next I was upright and standing next to my love. I leaned against him and put my face in the crook of his neck.

"You just missed the funniest thing I have ever seen in me entire life. I swear, Kane," I panted. "It was amazin'. It all started with Nico changin' a nappy, then Alec came in and boom, powder everywhere."

Kane vibrated with silent laughter as he hooked an arm around my waist to hold me upwards. "What happened to lead to them fighting like kids?"

"Alec cursed when the powder went all over him and Nico called him out on it. Alec hit Nico, Nico hit Alec, then they started rolling around on the floor like they're doin' now."

Kane laughed and stepped away from me and into Jax's bedroom. He put his foot on Nico's head and it halted all movement from the pair of wannabe wrestlers.

"I press down and it crushes your faces together, do you want to explain to your girls why you both have busted up faces when you go home?"

Alec wheezed. "I can't breathe! Get this fat bastard off of me right—"

"It's muscle!" Nico snapped and yanked on Alec's hair.

He literally reached up and pulled his brother's hair.

"Hey, enough!" Kane said on a laugh. "Both of you get up, you aren't setting a good example for your nephew. He is watching everything you're both doing right now."

Nico rolled off Alec and sat upright. He locked eyes with Jax who was lying down in his playpen in the corner of the room with his head turned in the direction of the brothers' brawl.

"You don't mind me teaching Uncle Alec a lesson, do you, buddy?" Nico cooed.

Jax screamed with delight at the attention and clapped his hands together making me laugh.

"You little traitor!" Alec coughed as he continued to lie on the floor.

I shook my head. "Are you okay, baby whisperer?"

"No, I was just *attacked*," Alec replied and shot daggers at Nico.

"What did you just call him?" Kane asked me as he picked Jax up.

Nico got to his feet and grumbled, "You don't want to know."

I smiled and said to Kane, "I'll tell you later."

He nodded his head and looked at his brothers, snorting.

"You both look ridiculous."

Nico grunted. "This wouldn't have happened if—"

"If *you* hadn't rushed me." Alec cut Nico off.

Nico stepped towards Alec, but Kane moved between them, holding Jax to his chest.

"Stop it."

Alec rolled his eyes, but focused on the powder on his clothes. Nico did the same and headed out of the room and went straight to the bathroom. Alec went to the kitchen and when I heard the water running I chuckled.

"When you're both cleaned up, you can get back in here and clean this room."

Nico said nothing, but Alec complained which only caused Kane to grin.

We walked into the kitchen when the door to our apartment opened again and in walked Ryder, Branna and Bronagh with Keela in tow. We all greeted them, but as soon as Nico entered the kitchen—less powdery—Bronagh focused solely on him.

"You know the way Branna's co-workers give me a scan every week for free when I pick her up on a Friday?"

Nico nodded his head and continued to wipe the baby powder from his clothes and skin.

"So I got the usual one today," she explained, her smile still in place. "And I'm measurin' at twenty-six weeks exactly."

"That's great, babe, so we're more than half way there?"

Bronagh nodded her head, her smile practically splitting her face.

"Why are you smiling at me like that?" Nico questioned.

"The technician made a little discovery too… about the gender."

Nico gasped. "I thought we agreed not to find out."

"We did," Bronagh nodded, "but she let it slip by mistake."

"You know the sex?" I asked.

Bronagh nodded her head. "So does Branna, she was next to me when the woman said it by accident."

Nico nervously licked his lips. "Tell me then."

"Are you sure? If you don't want to know then—"

"Bronagh." He cut her off. "Tell me."

Silence.

I glared at her for the unnecessary suspense and it caused her to laugh before she announced, "It's a girl."

I screamed with delight and jumped up and down which got Jax excited. He began to jump and scream in Kane's arms. Kane was frozen though, so were Alec and Ryder. They were all staring at Nico who was shockingly still.

"I'm sorry," he said. "I misheard you. I thought you said we were having a girl."

Bronagh blinked, taken aback by Nico's lack of... expression. "We *are* havin' a girl."

"You're false," Nico calmly said. "We're having all boys."

Bronagh bit back a grin. "Is that so?"

"Yeah, it is so," Nico countered.

"Well, honey, I don't know what to tell you because it's a baby girl in my belly... not a boy."

Nico paled and instantly turned to Kane. "I'll swap you my kid when it's born for Jax?"

"Dominic!" Branna chastised.

Kane stepped back and turned Jax away from his uncle's wild eyes. "Not a chance."

Nico suddenly looked to the ceiling and shouted, "I asked for a boy, not a girl! This wasn't part of the deal!"

Branna looked at me, bemused. "Who is he talkin' to?"

I looked to the ceiling then back to Branna and smiled. "Jesus."

Branna snickered and playfully shook her head at Nico. "Good luck seeking counsel, but don't get your hopes up... he never responds when I ask for help."

I don't know why, but I looked at Ryder when Branna spoke and I saw the weight her words held over him. He looked troubled that she was talking to God about something... he looked like he wanted to be the one she spoke to instead.

I let a small smile curve my lips.

He wasn't as disconnected as he wanted everyone to believe. He loved Branna, but for some strange reason he was fighting it, and I had no idea why.

"Are you jokin' right now?" Bronagh asked, her eyes welled with tears. "You better be because this isn't funny."

Nico sighed. "Don't get upset, it's just a shock... I really thought we would just have boys."

"Why?" Bronagh asked.

"Because Kane had a boy... it's not fair if I don't have one either."

Bronagh frowned. "Next time it might be a boy."

Nico placed his face in his hands. "What if she has sex really young? What if boys try it on with her in school like I did with you? Oh Christ, I need to sit down."

He pulled out a chair next to Ryder and sat down.

"She's not even born yet and you're thinking about—"

"We'll have to teach Jax to follow her around and scare off boys," Kane suggested.

Alec nodded his head. "Good idea, an inside man will help."

"Will help what?"

Ryder raised a brow. "Protecting a Slater girl from boys... what else?"

I placed my hand on my chest. "That is bloody adorable."

Bronagh smiled down at Nico before moving closer to him, placing her hand on his head. It took a second, but he turned and kissed her growing belly before looking up at her.

"A girl?"

"A girl."

He inhaled and exhaled. "We can deal with a girl."

He sounded like he was trying to convince himself.

"We could deal with twenty of them as long as we remain a team and don't be outsmarted."

"Twenty?" Nico spluttered. "Never. No fucking way."

Bronagh laughed.

I moved closer and gave her a long hug.

"Congratulations, babe."

She squeezed me back. "You could be carryin' a girl this time, too. You never know."

"Don't you *dare* wish that upon us, Bronagh Murphy!" Kane almost snarled.

I leaned down and kissed Nico's head. "You will be a great daddy no matter what."

His lip twitched. "Thanks, Ado."

"Where is Dame?" I asked Bronagh. "Does he know?"

She shook her head. "He is out lookin' for a job. We'll tell him later."

I nodded and moved over to Kane and Jax, taking Jax when he leaned towards me with outstretched arms. I took him into my arms, kissed his chubby cheeks and leaned against Kane's side. I frowned when *Big Phil* entered my mind.

I wanted to kick myself; I always thought about the disgusting son of a bitch when I felt thoroughly happy. It was a solid reminder that he remained out there and still wanted his vengeance. A part of me wanted him to attack and get it over with, while another part of me wanted to drag it out forever.

The latter was wishful thinking, because I knew Big Phil was like a snake. He was waiting to strike us when we least expected it. That knowledge caused me to live in constant fear.

I shook the thought away and looked to Ryder who was looking at Branna, but glanced away when she looked at him.

"What are we goin' to do about Branna and Ryder?" I murmured to Kane.

He turned his head and looked at the pair in question before he looked back to me and sighed.

"We can't do anything, babydoll." He frowned, his voice low. "They'll come out of this stronger as a couple or they'll break up and go their own ways."

That possibility made me feel sick.

"Ryder and Branna will constantly be around one another even if they break up; their siblings are going to marry eventually, and they'll share a niece or nephew."

Kane sighed. "Yeah, things will be tough if it comes to that."

Kane took Jax from me and walked over to Alec who instantly gave his nephew all his attention.

I smiled and looked from my boys to Ryder and Branna once more. Branna coughed after drinking some water, so Ryder absent-mindedly reached behind her and patted his hand between her shoulder blades to help her clear her throat, while he used his free hand to tap on the screen of his phone.

"Maybe there is hope for them after all," I murmured

"Of course there is," Bronagh's voice said from behind me. "They belong together. Both of them just need a whack on the head in order to realise it."

I turned around and found Keela and Bronagh huddled together as they approached me, their voices low.

"Enter *Ash Wade*." Keela devilishly smirked.

I blinked.

"Who is Ash Wade?" I asked, keeping my voice low, too.

"He is a new midwife that works the delivery suite with Branna," Bronagh informed me, her grin so wide it made her look scary happy.

I slowly nodded my head. "Okay, but how will Ash be the whack on the head Ryder and Branna both need to realise they're meant for one another?" I questioned.

Keela winked. "Let's just say after Branna told me a gorgeous new *male* midwife has an identical monthly shift to hers, I got to thinkin'. What does a Slater brother hate more than anythin' in this world when it comes to their women? What can't they stand sniffin' around what is theirs?"

A light bulb went off in my head, and I smirked.

"Other men."

"Exactly." Bronagh beamed. "And what do women of Slater

brothers love from other men?"

I felt guilty when I said, "Attention."

"But why?" Keela pushed.

I grinned. "Because attention from other men provokes *our* men to act like cavemen. We're theirs and they have no problem declarin' that to any man. Or woman."

"Not just a pretty face." Bronagh winked. "We don't need other men, but when they show us attention, we reap the benefits. I'm thinkin' if Ash shows Branna some attention it might knock Ryder upside the head and ring alarm bells that he might actually lose her. Branna will see his reaction and boom, back to their old ways they will go."

I tilted my head to the side and said, "You do realise how bad the outcome could turn out to be, don't you?"

Bronagh shrugged. "I'll have words with Ash, he'll know the score and will want to help. Everyone loves Branna and would do anythin' for her."

I sighed. "What if this goes really bad and they both kill us for interferin' in their relationship?"

Keela shrugged. "It can't go any worse than the way things are between them right now."

Are you sure about that?

I gnawed on my inner cheek. "I suppose."

"Does that mean you're in?" Bronagh asked, her eyebrows raised.

Was I?

I blinked. "What the hell, yeah, I'm in. I can't let you both do this without me, something would definitely go arseways."

Bronagh thrust her hips and squealed. "This is goin' to go perfectly," she announced, then turned around and strolled away with Keela in tow.

I lifted my hand and rubbed my neck, feeling very aware of the unsettling feeling that just took up residence in my stomach. I shook the feeling off and looked across the room to Ryder and Branna who were both on the opposite ends of the sofa, point blank ignoring each other.

I nervously swallowed, and to myself, I quietly murmured, "What's the worst that could happen?"

A voice in the back of my head whispered one word.

Enjoy a preview of,

RYDER

the next title in the Slater Brothers Series

CHAPTER ONE

Don't cry.

I repeated the thought over and over as I sat in Aideen and Kane's apartment and watched Bronagh interact with Dominic, his hand absentmindedly stroking her abdomen where their baby girl was growing.

I gnawed on my inner cheek as I looked away from the happy couple, and focused on the plasma screen TV on the wall facing me. My eyes watched the program that was showing, but my brain had no clue what was happening because it was elsewhere. I straightened up and hoped I didn't appear to be so out of sorts, but I wouldn't have been surprised if I did because I felt dreadful.

I was jealous.

I was green with envy every time I looked at Kane and Aideen with sweet baby Jax, but my heart broke when I watched how Dominic interacted with Bronagh. She was my little sister. I was a whole decade older than her and she had surpassed me on the journey to motherhood.

I had no doubt she would marry before me, too.

I hated that I felt so bitter towards my own blood. I was beyond happy for them, but I hated them a little at the same time. Her and Dominic were solid. They suited each other so well, and their love, though sometimes extremely intense, was true and forever binding.

The more I let myself think about them, the more depressed I felt when I looked at my own relationship.

I didn't think it could even be classed as a relationship anymore. Ryder and I, we both changed. Somewhere along the line, we stopped being nice to one another. We stopped loving one another. It started out as normal bickering that grew into full blown screaming contests. We weren't even at that angry stage anymore; we were at the silent one.

We ignored one another, and when we did interact, it wasn't pleasant.

I didn't know where we went wrong, but Ryder and I, we fell out of love. It pained me to admit that, but it was the truth. I loved him dearly, but I wasn't *in* love with him anymore, and that broke my heart because I had no idea how we got to the point we were at. I had no idea what I did wrong.

It was sorrowful.

I glanced to my left to where he was sat on Aideen's sofa. He was, as usual, tapping away on the screen of his phone and paying me no mind. I almost snickered when I remembered, many months ago, I used to feel hurt when he gave his phone more attention than me, but now I relished that the stupid device held his gaze, because I never wanted him to look at me and really see me like he used too, because he would see how weak I had become.

I didn't want him to see that I was broken.

I looked forward and then to my right. I picked up the bottle of water I got from Aideen's fridge when I came over. I uncapped the bottle, took a swig and swallowed down the cool liquid.

I widened my eyes when some of the water went down the wrong way and entered my lungs. I lowered my bottle and instantly began coughing as I lifted my hand and pressed it against my chest.

I jumped with fright when I felt a hand pressed against my back, and lightly tap away, helping me get the water up and regain my composure. I looked back to my left as Ryder retracted his hand away from me, without looking away from the screen of his phone.

I stared at him blankly, blindly.

I wasn't sure what to make of his kind gesture, which was terribly sad. He was my fiancé and I was beyond surprised that he touched me. He never touched me anymore. Not if he could help it anyway.

"Thank you," I said lowly to him.

He didn't look at me as he said, "Don't mention it."

Silence settled over us again, and my sadness returned.

I hated feeling so down.

I looked away from him and glanced around the room, my eyes landing on Aideen as Bronagh and Keela moved away from her, smirks in place on both of their pretty faces.

What were they up to now?

I lightly smiled to myself, and shook my head.

I looked down to my leg when it vibrated. I reached into my pocket and took out my phone, smiling when my co-workers name flashed across the screen.

Ash Wade.

He joined our crew at the hospital about ten weeks ago. He was a twenty-eight year old English man who moved over from London when he was twenty years old and loved it so much that he never went back home.

Ash was a hoot. He made me laugh on days that I thought I could do nothing but cry. He talked to me, and he listened to me talk. A lot. He became quite a good friend of mine, and I was very thankful to have met him at a point in my life when I need a pick-me-up.

Ash was pure light; he would brighten up anyone's day.

I slid my finger across the green blob on the screen, then brought the phone to my ear.

"What do you want?" I asked, grinning.

Ash snorted through the receiver. "It's a good thing I didn't misdial a hotline number and ask for phone sex when you fired *that* loaded question my way."

I joyfully laughed, the sound surprising me and others around me. I looked forward when I felt many sets of eyes on me, but only one set that caused me to tense up.

His eyes.

We had grown apart, but I could never seem to shake the sensation that came over me when he looked at me. The moment his eyes locked onto my body, I became hyper aware of every movement I made.

"Branna?" Ash's voice called out. "You there, Angel?"

I couldn't help but playfully roll my eyes.

Ash decided to label me with the nickname Angel when the grandfather of one of our patients a few weeks back kept calling me it when he addressed me. I asked him to drop it, but he hasn't, and it had seemed to stick.

"I'm here," I replied. "Sorry, just zoned out for a second."

"No worries," Ash chirped then lowered his voice. "You won't *believe* what happened on the ward today after you went home."

Ash worked the delivery suite with me, and bar a few extra hours here and there, we had an identical roster.

"If you tell me the patient in suite four that screamed bloody murder all day randomly stopped when I walked off the ward, then I'm goin' to curse her."

Ash's deep laughter filled my ear, and it warmed my hurt heart.

"No, she was *still* screaming when I left ... even though she got her epidural and was numb from the waist down."

I giggled. "There's always one who goes overboard."

Ash grunted. "You're telling me."

I chortled. "What happened?"

"The lady in suite one, you know, the hot redhead with *massive* tits?"

Ash was brilliant, but he was still such a man.

I good-naturedly shook my head. "Yeah, what about her?"

"She shit herself as she pushed. Her husband freaked out not knowing what was happening and fainted, knocked into the bed and caused shit to literally fly *everywhere*."

I fell onto the arm of the sofa as laughter erupted out of me.

"I swear," Ash laughed with me. "It's both hilarious *and* disgusting."

I wiped under my eyes with my free hand when tears of laughter fell.

"Did she deliver fine?" I asked, automatically switching to midwife mode. "And the husband, is he okay?"

"Both are fine. She had a boy, but I doubt the husband will step foot inside the delivery ward ever again. He made his wife swear to bring her mother in with her in the future."

I continued to laugh. "I bet you all had a right laugh about that."

"We did," Ash confirmed. "Sally almost wet herself from laughing after she got the baby cleaned up."

Sally was the fifty-seven year old 'mother' of the delivery suite. I wasn't on shift with her very often, but when I was, she cracked me up with tales from her younger days.

I shook my head, smiling joyfully. "I can't say I'm sorry I missed it. I've fifty-three deliveries running with nothing other than regular bodily fluids and a baby poppin' out. Thank God."

"You know your first patient on shift tomorrow will shit just for that comment?"

"Bite me!" I quipped.

Ash gleefully laughed. "I'll see you in the morning."

He picked me up on our way to work since I sold my car last year and Ryder always needed his Rover.

"Yep, I'll see you then."

I pocketed my phone and yawned before looking to Ryder who was still busy with his phone.

"Do you plan on being here long?" I asked, not looking at his hands.

He glanced at me and shook his head. "You wanna leave now?"

I nodded. "I'm on shift at eight in the mornin' and want to go to sleep early."

Ryder nodded his head. "I'll see if Damien wants a ride back."

I absentmindedly smiled as I thought about my boy. He helped bring some life back into me when he came home and moved back into the house. He made it feel less empty.

I blinked when Ryder stood up from the chair. He offered me his hand and, for a moment, I was hesitant about putting my hand in his. I shook it off and slid my hand into his large calloused one.

I licked my lips when he pulled me to my feet, but frowned when he released my hand and move passed me, heading towards his brothers. I tried not to let it get me down, but I couldn't help it. I missed him. I missed being close to him. I missed sex with him.

I couldn't remember the last time we were intimate, and I hated it.

I said goodbye to the girls, the brothers, and winked at Kane as he brought Jax into his room to put him to bed. I congratulated my sister and Dominic on finding out the gender of their baby once more, and followed Ryder out of Aideen's apartment, down the hallway and into the elevator.

"Dame will be home later," Ryder said as he hit the button for the ground floor.

The doors closed shut, encasing us together. I felt him look at me, so I kept my eyes dead ahead, making sure my body was tensed and non-moving, too.

"Who were you talking to on the phone?" he asked me, his voice so low I barely heard him.

I was a little annoyed that he asked me an invasive question when he never answered any of mine. I wanted to counter with multiple questions of my own, asking where he went every night when he thought I was asleep and why he was on his phone all the time, but I had no energy for a fight.

He wouldn't answer me if I asked anyway; he never did.

"Just Ash who works the delivery suite with me."

Out of the corner of my eye, I saw Ryder nod. He had never met Ash, so I had no idea what was going through his mind with my response.

"Are you okay?" he randomly asked.

I was so surprised at the question that I looked at him with raised eyebrows and said, "Yes, why wouldn't I be?"

He shrugged, staring down at me, his eyes non-blinking. "You barely cracked a smile when Bronagh was announcing she was having a girl."

Because I did my happy dance back at the hospital when she found out.

I looked forward. "I had a long day at work, I'm just tired."

"Too tired to be happy for your sister?"

How dare he!

"I *am* happy for her. I don't need to be all up in her face to be happy for her, Ryder."

Silence.

"It seems to me like you're a little bit ..."

"A little bit what?" I pressed.

The door of the elevator opened just as Ryder said, "Jealous."

I stepped out of the elevator, politely nodded to the security man that manned the lobby desk, and quickly walked in the direction of the main entrance.

"Branna?" Ryder groaned. "Look, wait a second."

I didn't. I picked up my pace and almost sprinted out of the apartment complex. When I got outside, I nodded to the security guards at the doors and headed straight for Ryder's Land Rover that was parked in-between Dominic and Alec's cars.

I rushed to the passenger door and stared at the handle until I heard Ryder sigh and press on the car key, unlocking the doors. I gripped the handle, pulled the door open and got up into the car, slamming the door shut behind me.

"Damn it, Branna," Ryder complained when he got into the driver's seat. "Don't take your bad mood out on my car."

Fuck you and your stupid car.

"I wouldn't be in a bad mood had you not said somethin' so ..."

"So what?"

"*Insensitive!*" I finished.

"Insensitive," Ryder repeated and turned his body to face me. "*How* is me saying you're jealous of Bronagh having a girl insensitive?"

I couldn't even look at him.

"You aren't stupid. Think about it and I'm sure you'll realise why."

Ryder didn't move a muscle as he continued to stare at me.

"You *are* jealous," he murmured then gasped. "You want a baby?"

I looked out the window, not answering him.

"Branna," he pressed. "You want a baby?"

Without looking at him I said, "I've wanted a baby for *years*, I just never said anythin' to you to push the issue because so much bullshit has happened to our families, and being the oldest pair we had to push everythin' aside and make sure everyone was okay. We're the parental figures. We make sure everyone else is doin' good before we even consider lookin' at our own needs."

Ryder was silent as I spoke so I pressed on.

"You *know* I love kids and I probably would have had a few before I met you, but havin' a life was put on hold when me parents died. I had to focus on Bronagh, not me, *her*. Bein' a midwife was me dream, it's the one thing I allowed meself to want. It's why I worked me arse off to become one in me late twenties whilst raisin' a bratty teenager."

I glanced at him as he continued to remain silent.

"Do you think we're at a point where we should have a kid?" he asked, and I heard the doubt laced throughout his voice.

It killed me, but I agreed with him.

"No, we aren't in the position to raise a dog, let alone a child."

Ryder faced forward and jammed his key into the ignition and started up his car.

"Besides," he quipped, "we'd actually have to *fuck* in order to get you pregnant."

His anger was expected.

I flattened my hands out on my thighs and resisted the urge to ball them into fists.

"We probably would if *you* didn't go off every single night to do God knows what."

The silent 'or who' was implied, but the words never left my lips because I was terrified if it turned out to be a 'who' that was the reason for him leaving every night.

I didn't think I would be able to handle that, and decided I was better off not knowing. My sister, and the other girls, would smack me around for resorting to this way of thinking, but they didn't know what my home life or relationship with Ryder was like.

They thought they knew, but they didn't.

"Don't feed me that bullshit," Ryder growled as he pulled out of the space. "I'm home a lot and you *still* never put out. You left our bed too sleep up in Dominic's old room, the furthest away from me that you can be in *our* house."

I felt disgusted.

"Me purpose on this Earth isn't to fuck you whenever you see fit."

"No," Ryder agreed, "but it'd be nice if I could hit it at least once a fucking week. I haven't touched you in months. I'd settle for fucking spooning at this point."

He spoke of me like I was nothing more than a sexual object.

"And whose fault is that?" I bellowed, throwing my hands in the air. "*You've* pulled away from me. We don't talk, we don't laugh, we don't do anythin' but fight with one another and it's *your* bloody fault. *You* have landed us in this rut, and the sad thing is I don't even know why! I don't know what you do when you leave the house every night, or why you're always on your phone, and it's pathetic that I've just accepted it, but I'm too tired. I fight with you all the time, I'm too exhausted to do anythin' else."

I turned my head and looked out the window of the car, willing the tears in my eyes not to fall. I didn't want to cry, I was sick of crying.

"I've told you I'm takin' care of some things. That's all you need to know."

I closed my eyes, gutted he still wouldn't share his secrets with me.

"I don't believe you, Ryder."

"Then I don't know what to tell you, Branna."

"How about the truth for once?" I countered. "Just tell me where you go and what you do."

His hands tightened around the steering wheel as we approached our street.

"I can't tell you, you wouldn't understand."

I looked down to my thighs and swallowed.

"I can't understand if you don't help me to."

Ryder grunted as he pulled into the car parking space in front of our house, putting the car in park. "This is on me, okay? It's nothing for you to worry about, and you *will* worry if I tell you, and I don't want that to happen. We're all under a lot of pressure with Big Phil still out there; my business doesn't need me added to that."

He got out of the car, closed the door and walked up the pathway and into our house, leaving me on my own with my thoughts.

"I can't do this anymore," I said aloud, forcing myself to hear the words.

We couldn't continue on the path we were on. Something had to change, and in that moment I knew exactly what I had to do to start the healing process for the many wounds that had been cut open and exposed over the last few years.

I had to make a change. I had to separate myself from the very being that wounded me so ... even if he didn't mean to.

I squeezed my eyes shut as pain struck. The remaining fragments of my willowed heart shattered into a million pieces as I made a life changing decision. A decision that would affect not only me, but my family and friends, too.

I reached out and blindingly gripped onto the dashboard of the car to stop myself from collapsing as my mind whispered what I needed to do to be free.

I had to break up with Ryder.

Don't cry.

OTHER TITLES

FROZEN

SLATER BROTHERS SERIES:

DOMINIC
BRONAGH
ALEC
KEELA
KANE

ACKNOWLEDGEMENTS

I love reaching the acknowledgments section of a novel or novella; it means I've just added a new notch to my book belt.

Aideen is the sixth book in my *Slater Brothers* series, and that puts me at the halfway mark in this insane journey between the brothers and their ladies.

That. Is. Insane.

I say this after every book I write, but I honestly can't wrap my head around how far I've come with this series, and it is *still* going strong. I'm so blessed, and so very thankful to all those who make it possible.

My daughter, I love you more than humanly possible. You are my life. All of what I do and continue to do, I do for you. I love you to Neptune and back.

My PA—Jill. You're a superstar, woman, and I love you dearly.

Yessi, I don't know where to start with you. You're always there for me, and you continue to be one of the few people who I truly consider are pure light. Love you, bitch.

My Mary, I love everything about you. You have quickly become one of my favourite people. You. Are. Brilliant.

Jen—the main woman behind JaVa Editing. Thank you so much for revamping editing for me. You completely put me at ease during the editing process on *Aideen*. Your comments and random messages cracked me up, and your input was on point. I can't wait to work with you again.

Nicola Rhead & KMS Freelance Editing, thank you both for

proofreading *Aideen*. I truly appreciate it.

L.J. Anderson—the master behind Mayhem Cover Creations, thank you for creating yet *another* cover that I am in love with.

Julie—the boss behind JT Formatting, thank you for prettifying *Aideen*.

Last, but never least, my readers. I don't know where I would be without all of you, but I know I definitely wouldn't be releasing my sixth book in the series if it weren't for each and every one of you. Thank you for everything. You continue to make my dreams possible.

<3

About the Author

L.A. Casey is a New York Times and USA Today bestselling author who juggles her time with her mini-me and writing. She was born, raised and currently resides in Dublin, Ireland. She enjoys chatting with her readers, who love her humour and Irish accent as much as her books.

Casey's first book *Dominic*, was independently published in 2014 and became an instant success on Amazon. Now a hybrid author, she is both traditionally and independently published and is represented by Mark Gottlieb from Trident Media Group.

To read more about this author,
visit her website at www.lacaseyauthor.com

Made in the USA
Charleston, SC
08 May 2016